To the Point

Short Tales of a Wandering Mind

Romana Capek-Habeković

Table of Contents

The Garage Sale

I heard a knock on my door and rushed to open it. I saw PJ dressed in light blue jeans and a striped V-neck top that she usually wore when she went grocery shopping at Great Scott.

"Hi PJ, no need nothing. Dave goes to Great Scott yesterday," I said in my 3-month-old English.

"No, I am not going grocery shopping. Let me take you around our neighborhood. You probably didn't see it all. There are some nice houses around."

I quickly put on my white cotton cardigan, and before closing the door I shouted to my husband who was shaving in the bathroom.

"I am going with PJ to see other Taylor's streets. Take care of Marko, I'll be back soon.

I sat in PJ's old Pinto full of crumbs on the passenger side and discarded McDonald's paper cups and Styrofoam containers on the floor behind me. I wasn't surprised seeing the messy interior of her car because it reflected her overall lax attitude toward neatness. Her apartment was always in disarray with children's toys scattered across the lime green, stained wall-to-wall carpet, dirty clothes spilled over the edge of a large hamper, clean ones dumped on one of the beds waiting to be folded, and the kitchen sink was consistently full of dirty dishes. None of it bothered PJ because she preferred sitting next to the window, playing her guitar, and singing. I didn't judge her lack of household skills because she was the first neighbor who introduced herself and invited me for a coffee in her apartment, and I appreciated that. Moving from the former Yugoslavia to the United States was a traumatic experience for me on every level imagined—from not speaking English, to not driving, to being unfamiliar with the culture, and the list goes on. PJ was my first guide through the great unknown.

While driving, PJ told me about the offer she had gotten from the nearby bar to sing there twice a week. She had a beautiful, melodic voice especially suited to country music and spiritual songs. People who visited the bar were Taylor residents who were used to listening to that kind of music from the jukebox while drinking beer and socializing after work. The owner figured out that by having live entertainment more customers would come. PJ taught herself how to strum and memorize her singing repertoire by listening to tapes. In spring and summer with her windows wide open, I would hear her singing accompanied by the soft sound of her classical instrument. She aspired to become a recorded musician, but her dream never materialized because of the life circumstances she was thrown into from an unwed teenage pregnancy to several relocations in search of a job, to a marriage to a functional alcoholic, Eddie, ten years older than her and a father of two young men from his earlier relationship.

PJ drove slowly showing me homes where several people from her St. Constance Catholic Church lived. She would meet them after each Sunday mass that she attended with her daughter Lisa, baby Michael, and Eddie if he was awake after his Saturday binging on Budweiser.

"PJ, why people sell garage, car stay on the street?"

"What do you mean?"

"I see sign 'Garage Sale.'"

"They are not selling their garages. They are selling items that they don't want or need any longer. You can find some really good things. I bought our black leather sofa for $10 from an old couple moving to a retirement home. Would you like us to browse through one of those garages that are open?"

"No, I have no money with me."

"You don't have to buy anything. It's fun just looking!"

I was grateful that PJ got used to my broken English and never made me repeat what I was saying. On the other hand, I tried to grasp her slang-free English and perfectly formulated sentences.

PJ parked on the street behind a maroon station wagon. The homeowners put garden tools, children's tricycles, and old furniture on the driveway. Inside the garage they had foldable tables full of dishes, mismatched silverware, games, men's and women's accessories, and clothes no longer in vogue. The only other customers in there were four women from the station wagon. They came carrying large garbage bags as if being prepared to fill them up with bargain items. The women quickly moved between tables, eyeing all vendibles. They seemed mostly interested in glittery serving dishes and wine glasses with green and ochre stems from another era. I noticed that they bought two sets of those in addition to vintage-looking dessert plates. Despite being open, the garage still smelled mildewy, probably from the clothes packed in boxes that were left in the humid basement before being brought up for the garage sale. The whole scene of displayed and discarded objects and four women rushing to buy whatever they could find I saw as a scavenger hunt for those who delighted in owning other people's junk. I decided then not ever to buy anything preowned, especially not clothes.

We returned to the car and cruised for a while throughout Taylor's winding streets. The sun was high and heated the containers with the leftover hamburger bites. The Pinto began to stink, and PJ rolled down all the windows.

"Thank you, PJ, for taking me to garage sale."

"You are welcome! Next time, we will go to an estate sale," she said, and her dimpled smile made me happy.

I learned later that estate sales, mostly in the upscale neighborhoods, attracted a more sophisticated clientele who were looking for brand names and rare antiques. Neither PJ nor I belonged to that group.

Paper Flowers

In 1974 I was a new émigré from the former Yugoslavia. My husband was accepted into the residency program at Oakwood Hospital in Dearborn. He arrived three months before me and our seventeen-month-old son. His friend, J.G., from the Medical School in Zagreb, already in his second year at the same hospital, recommended him. I was the follower who didn't speak English and the only source of my knowledge about the American culture and social practices stemmed from having watched Hollywood made movies. I knew that regardless of my college degree, I would be a homemaker and look after our son.

The first people I met when I arrived were J.G. and his wife, Lada. She introduced me to the wives of other residents who were trained in different specialties. They were her neighbors living in small ranch-style houses across from the hospital. Having been a recent emigrant herself, she knew that I felt out of place and outside of my comfort zone. She told me that it took her an entire year to get accustomed to the diverse aspects of her new existence. Having a degree in English made her acclimatization much easier. Mine was in Italian, thus useless at first. I also felt terribly lonely, not knowing anybody in the apartment building where the hospital rented one for us. I missed my friends and Zagreb (the Croatian capital), the city in which I was born and raised. Our housing complex was in Taylor, a small city west of Detroit and south of 94, famous as the founding location of Hungry Howie's Pizza. When Lada called me one day, I was happy to hear what she said.

"Bonney is inviting you to a craft party in her house. It's tomorrow evening. You only need to bring cheese and crackers. I'll bring crepes. Your husband can drive you to our house, and I'll take you back."

I was looking forward to seeing Lada's friends again and spending the evening in the company of adults. The hostess was a petite dark-haired woman with a child-like sounding high pitched voice and a plastered smile. Lada liked her because of her easygoing nature, optimism, cordiality, and especially her willingness to babysit her daughter while she was shopping for clothes. In addition to the three of us, there was also Monica from the house adjacent to Lada's; Candy, a nurse working at Lyn Hospital who also lived in Taylor; Carol, a stay-home mom; and Laura, a Utah Mormon, who brought a jar of her homemade preserve as a gift for Bonney. The last person who came was Pat, a high school English teacher in Detroit whom I had not met before. Our introductory exchanges cemented life-long friendship.

"Hello, I am Pat, and a ballet dancer. What do you do?"

"I am a teacher but stay home now."

I misunderstood what she said her profession was, and thought that she was a belly dancer, which I found interesting and refreshing. Pat was a bit taller than I, slender yet muscular, with thick reddish hair that reached her shoulders and beautiful blue eyes sparkling through her glasses. Her laugh was contagious, and when she spoke all eyes were on her. I felt an instant kinship with her. I appreciated that she quickly recognized my struggle to follow the women's chatter, thus when she talked, she would simplify her sentences and lower her speed. She also rushed to take a seat at the kitchen table next to me, as if wanting to make sure that I would understand Bonney's directions as to what to do with the colorful streamers, foot long metal sticks, and scissors for each person spread across it. I couldn't even guess what we were supposed to do with these items.

"Bonney, show us how you made your bouquet. It is beautiful!" Monica, the tall blond woman with Farrah Fawcett's hairstyle, complimented Bonny's craft project.

I followed her gaze to the vase on the coffee table full of flowers made from streamers. I never saw anything that ugly in my entire life.

"Oh, thank you, Monica. I'll show you how to make them; it's really easy."

I replicated Bonney's steps from cutting a fourteen-inch-long red streamer to rolling it around her thumb to twisting the lower portion of it and separating layers to form the shape of a flower.

She attached the twisted part to the metal stick, and proudly said, "Voilà! Easy, peasy! I bought enough streamers so you can make as many flowers as you wish."

Lada and Candy finished their second flower, Monica was struggling to attach hers to the metal stick, and Laura was fussing with separating the layers. I was still working on my first flower, when Bonney pulled a gallon of Carlo Rossi's burgundy out of the fridge.

"Hey girls, how about some wine, you all are too serious?"

She placed a glass in front of each of us except for Laura, whose Mormon beliefs followed the Word of Wisdom as their commandments, which banned the consumption of alcohol and coffee. Decades later, the Church issued a statement allowing their followers to drink coffee and tea.

"An excellent idea, Bonney!" Lada was the first to accept the offer.

The more our group drank, the more the conversation around the table became livelier. I understood half of what the others said. To cover up my meager knowledge of English I smiled and nodded as if I was following it in full. The initial colloquy focused on children and household chores. The subsequent topics were the hospital gossip and the bashing of their husbands' families. I wanted to blend in and contribute with my own narrative, but realized that besides lacking the fluency in English, I had nothing in common with these women, the exception being Lada with whom I shared a country of origin. They grew up in a culture alien to me. I didn't understand their references to various aspects of American life from food to sports, to fashion, and raising kids. That evening nobody talked about movies, books they were reading, and politics, topics widely discussed at any gathering with my old friends. I wrongfully generalized that Americans either avoided controversial topics, such as the innerworkings of different governments and the impact of diverse religions on the global landscape or were simply not interested in them. This is a common mistake emigrants make to compare their native culture to their new one and consider the latter inferior. Their other erroneous assumption is to judge the pulse of an entire country based on communication with only a small group such as the one I was part of that evening.

We proceeded to roll streamers into colorful flowers. The handiest person was Carol. She must have done different craft projects before. I made three flowers—red, white, and green—the colors of the Italian flag. As the evening progressed, the gaiety of the women grew as the gallon of burgundy geared toward its bottom. The cheese and crackers, as well as Lada's jam-filled crepes, were also gone.

"Girls, it is ten o'clock. Let's finish your last flower." Bonney rushed us when she heard her husband's car in the driveway. He was returning from his afternoon shift at the hospital.

The neighborhood women were tipsy and held onto each other while walking to their nearby houses, and others who had to drive drank several glasses of water before getting in their cars.

"You don't need to call your husband to pick you up. I can drive you home," Pat offered.

"Thank you!" I was grateful for her suggestion because my husband would have to take our son with him, and neither of them would be happy about a night ride.

"If you need help with learning English, I'll be happy to explain the basics to you. Better yet, why don't I pick you up next Saturday and bring you to my house for a coffee or tea?"

"Thank you! I like that."

Pat dropped me off in front of the entrance of our apartment. Her hug instead of a customary, "Bye," surprised me and made me feel better and worse at the same time because I was certain that she pitied me, and yet her embrace if just for a second lessened my lonesomeness.

"How was your evening?" my husband asked.

"It was OK," I answered laconically, putting the paper flowers on the kitchen table.

I quickly brushed my teeth and entered our bedroom without checking on our sleeping son. I closed the door and slid under the comforter. I pulled it all the way to my chin and began to sob. I hoped that my husband would not hear me, but he did.

"Why are you crying? What happened?"

"I want to go home! I don't want to make paper flowers as if I am a mental patient."

Stunned for a few seconds, he could not find the right words to console me.

"Don't go to these gatherings anymore if they upset you."

The next time Bonney kindly invited me to crochet covers for toilet paper with the same group, I found an excuse. I heard from Lada that Pat didn't join them either. I am sure that my aversion to craft projects today originated from that evening.

Driving Lessons

As a recent transplant from the former Yugoslavia, I didn't know how to drive. I lived in a city with a well-developed public tram and bus transportation system, which I used when I needed to go places further east or west from my parents' downtown apartment. My father owned a light blue Fiat 750 but didn't allow me to get a driver's license because he was afraid that I might wreck his car. He himself drove it only at weekends because he preferred going on foot to his work. I was also able to walk to most of my destinations.

The first-floor neighbor, PJ, a newcomer from Massachusetts, was the first person to welcome me upon my moving into a two-story, red brick house situated within the large Taylor residential complex. She would often invite me for an afternoon coffee and patiently listen to my attempts to speak English. By way of those meetings of ours I learned about different aspects of American culture. Her percolated coffee looked like tea to me because of its light brown color. She would bring a gallon of milk out of the fridge in case I couldn't drink it black as she did. I would ask her for some sugar to make it taste better. Fifty years later, I still cannot drink American coffee black.

PJ invited my husband, our twenty-month-old son, and me to Thanksgiving dinner, a novel culinary experience for us. She pulled out of the oven a 16-pound turkey and placed it on a huge wooden tray. Her husband, Eddie, expertly carved it while sipping his Budweiser. A lit cigarette was hanging in the corner of his mouth. I was certain that some ashes would fall on the meat, but they didn't. PJ opened a can of jellied cranberry sauce and placed the bowl of premade mashed potatoes in the middle of the table. She proceeded to boil green beans and to heat up gravy from another can. I recognized the stuffing from the bags I saw at Great Scott. She just moistened it with some warm water. She also served half frozen buns and a stick of margarin.

There were six of us sitting at the table—PJ, Eddie, ten years older than her, Lisa her four-year-old daughter, and my family. I remember only putting side dishes on my plate because I never liked poultry. The conversation was surprisingly lively because my husband's English was very good, and Eddie became eloquent after several beers and described his military service in Italy. PJ inserted her comments once in a while, I mostly listened, lacking the necessary vocabulary for a meaningful dialogue, and the children sat quietly eating only buns smeared with margarine. This was our first Thanksgiving.

"That went OK," my husband said after we returned to our apartment.

"Agree, but I'll never forget the size of that turkey. Ours used to weigh the most 3kg."

The first snow fell in December and buried our blue Mustang under several feet of frozen snow. In the morning, my husband spent an hour digging it out to be able to drive to work. While visiting PJ for our daily dose of caffeine, I sat across the large window in her living room and saw icicles reaching down from the second-floor windows.

"PJ, I am thirsty," I uttered one of my English sentences. Most of my English 101 was based on food and drinks.

Holding a glass of water, she asked me, "Would you like some ice?"

"No, thank you."

I couldn't believe why anybody would consume ice-cold water while the outside temperature was below zero and the wind chilled bones and cracked lips. The woolen coat I brought with me in one of my two suitcases was not warm enough, and I had to buy a puffer jacket. The popularity of ice-cold water was an American staple, somebody told me later.

When spring came around, I decided that it was time for me to learn how to drive because I felt trapped in our two-bedroom apartment. I also realized that it was a necessity for my immersion into a new way of living. I mentioned that to my husband, and he agreed that it was a good idea.

"I will teach you. It's easy because you don't need to shift gears, just press the accelerator and the brakes," he said.

Easier said than done. During my first driving lesson with him, he was disappointed that I was not able to back out of our assigned parking place despite not being any cars parked on either side of us. When I finally accomplished that, he ordered me to slowly exit the house complex and turn left to the street that led to the subdivision with the small ranch homes and dilapidated trucks parked in front of one-car garages.

"Why are you slowing down? Just press on the pedal and drive," he raised his voice.

"Don't yell! You make me nervous. I don't want you to teach me how to drive." I stopped the car and handed him the keys.

"OK, sign up for driving school. They can teach you better." He sounded irritated.

The very next day I called PJ.

"PJ, can you teach me how to drive? I really must learn it. Dave doesn't have patience for instructing me."

"Sure, when do you want to go?"

"How about this weekend? He doesn't need the car."

"Sounds good! Just knock on my door when you are ready. I am free on Saturday and on Sunday."

"Dave, could you please hand me the car keys. PJ is going to teach me how to drive," I said to him the following Saturday.

"Be careful! If you damage it, I cannot go to work," was his main concern, which reminded me of my father.

I sat in our 1974 Mustang with PJ on the passenger side.

"First, adjust your seat and the rear mirror," she calmly instructed me.

"Before putting the shift in reverse, you have to make sure that nobody is behind you. Now, press lightly on the gas and turn the wheel to face the street in front of us."

I followed her instructions and began to drive below the speed limit throughout the subdivision.

"You are doing great!" She smiled and clapped after we returned to my parking spot.

"Let's go again each day after your husband returns from work and you have the car. Days are long now, and you would not be driving in the dark."

After one week of driving in the neighborhood, PJ convinced me that I was ready to enter Telegraph Road, one of the busiest in the area.

"It is not busy on Saturday morning; let's go this weekend!"

"PJ, I cannot. I am not sure. There a multiple lanes and cars passing all around me. I will have to drive faster."

"Oh, come on, don't be a chicken!"

Either my faith in her teaching methods or her trust in me persuaded me that I could drive on the freeway. PJ was right. As soon as I entered Telegraph, an unexpected calm washed over me. I held the wheel in a tight grip and pressed harder on the accelerator to reach the minimally allowed speed. PJ was beaming with pride. I still wonder how brave or stupid we both were for such a bold move that put us in harm's way. Just a small, unpredicted traffic related event could throw out my concentration and ability to react to it fast. I guess we were young and thought we were invincible.

"I think that you are ready to get your driver's license. Here is the booklet with traffic rules that you need to study for your written test before the driving test. If you don't understand something, I'll explain it to you. Don't worry, it's not hard."

"PJ, I am not sure about that. The test plus my driving, God knows if I can make it!"

I began to read the booklet and realized that I understood more English than I gave to myself credit for.

"PJ, I am ready to go to the Secretary of State for that driver's license!"

"Good girl! Let's do it!" She was a true trooper.

PJ waited while I was taking the written portion of my exam. When I handed it completed to the clerk, she read it, and routinely said, "You are OK. I'll call the driving instructor to take you on the road."

I sent a thumbs up in PJ's direction, and instead of remaining seated, she headed toward me.

"I told you that you would pass the test. I just want to have a few words with the driving instructor. I see him coming."

I had no idea what she wanted to tell him.

"Hello, I am her friend. She just immigrated to the States and barely speaks any English. I am not sure that she will understand your driving directions. Can I sit in the car with you in case she needs my help?"

"Absolutely not! If she cannot understand me, she shouldn't get a license until she learns English," he adamantly refused PJ's plea.

That was the first time that I saw PJ nervous. It was my turn to reassure her that everything would be OK – I again raised my thumb in the air, and a broad smile crossed her face. We were partners in this adventure.

"Go to the counter where they will take your photo for the license," the instructor said slowly and loudly as if making sure that I understood him.

PJ ran toward me, we hugged and jumped up in the air happy to have reached our goal – to Americanize me in the fastest feasible way – by getting my driver's license.

A Doggie Bag

I left half of my pastrami sandwich and potato chips on my plate. Their portions were large, and I was unable to eat them all. The waitress came to the table where I was sitting with four of my recently met friends and asked me, "Would you like a doggie bag?"

"No, thank you, I don't have a dog!"

It was obvious that she had a hard time containing herself not to burst out laughing, but my friends went ahead. Since the woman looked puzzled, one of them explained the context of why I refused the offered doggie bag.

"My friend has been in the States just a few months, and the concept of a doggie bag was unknown in Yugoslavia where she comes from."

In subsequent years, I got used to generous portions of food served in American restaurants, but on those rare occasions when I couldn't clear my plate, I would happily accept the doggie bag for tomorrow's lunch. On a few occasions when my entree was substandard and I left most of it untouched, I was tempted to tell the server to bring me the doggie bag because my Labrador would eat it. Language is such an irreplaceable tool of communication but sometimes fails to decipher the cultural context of the words.

Eddie

I heard through the heating vents Karin's loud voice coming from the basement. Her apartment was on the first floor below ours. We lived in one of the identical-looking houses in the residential complex in Taylor. Each built with red bricks, energy deficient cheap aluminum framed windows, and a shared basement passable through unlocked doors between them. I decided to investigate what happened that would make a mild mannered, soft-spoken, petite woman yell at the top of her lungs. I descended two flights of the stairs to reach the basement entrance.

"Dammit! What should I do now? Throw it all in the garbage or wash it? Goddamn!"

"Karin, what is going on?" I asked her from afar.

"Somebody shit on my clean laundry that I left in the basket for a few minutes because I heard the phone ringing in my apartment."

"Oh, my goodness! This is terrible!"

I came over to her and saw the laundry basket filled with all whites and a large pile of feces on top of them.

"What are you going to do?"

"I guess I'll first hose everything in the bathtub and then wash it again on hot. I bet that the new neighbor from the house adjacent to ours left her main entrance unlocked. That enabled one or more intruders to enter the building. I saw her when she was unloading her groceries. She looked trashy in her stained top and messy hair. Have you met her?"

"No, I didn't. You should notify the management about what happened."

A week or so passed when I descended to the first floor intending to proceed to the basement to put our laundry in the washing machine. I went in the evening because at that time both washers were usually free. Thinking about Karin's incident, I placed a large kitchen knife on the top of my laundry for protection in case I encountered a menacing-looking stranger. As I stood on the top of the stairs that led to the basement, I heard muffled male voices. That spooked me, and I decided to knock on PJ's and Eddie's door before heading downstairs. Their apartment was across from Karin's. I banged several times before Eddie finally opened it. She was not home. He appeared disheveled as if awake despite it being only eight o'clock. His unbuttoned, checkered flannel shirt exposed his worn-out white T-shirt. His face was red and puffy, typical of alcoholics that I had met in the past. A few of them were members of my extended family.

"What's the matter, neighbor?" he asked me in a bit halted and slurred voice. I was sure that he didn't remember my name. His alcohol infused breath reached me. He must have finished his usual six-pack after work and fallen asleep.

"Eddie, I heard voices from the basement. Could you please stay by the open door until I put my laundry in the washer? I am alone because my husband is on call."

"Sure, I'll be right here."

I trusted that he would keep his word. He didn't offer to accompany me to the basement, and I thought that it was for the best because being intoxicated he could have fallen while going down the stairs and broken some bones.

My apprehension grew with each step. When I opened the basement door, I found myself facing two young men puffing away on a shared marijuana joint. They were in their early twenties, skinny and tall. They could not hide their surprise seeing me because they counted on the basement being vacant in the evening. They must have been familiar with the residents' times of using it.

"What are you doing? Who let you in? We are families with children here!" I said it loudly to calm my nerves.

They didn't answer, just stared at my knife visible in plain sight because I was purposely standing under the nearest light bulb. I saw fear in their eyes. They threw the joint on the cement floor, quickly stamping on it to extinguish it, and ran to the next exit. They disappeared in a matter of seconds.

It took me a few minutes to compose myself and place the laundry in the washer that stood near the main house heater. While closing the top, I noticed newspapers spread out behind the furnace, McDonald's wrappings, and soda cans, obvious signs that somebody was staying there when the weather outside worsened. I left the basement and wanted to thank Eddie for being on guard in case I needed help, but I found his door closed. I was certain that he forgot he ever talked to me.

The next day I told Karin about my basement encounter and about the discovery behind the heater.

"Whoever slept there must have soiled your laundry."

"It sounds about right! I would advise that you never go to the basement again when you hear unknown voices! You could have been hurt or worse! Your knife would not save you when dealing with people on drugs."

"Oh, they were just kids! They didn't mean any harm. I don't understand how PJ can stand seeing Eddie drunk every day."

"As long as he keeps his job as a computer repairman. Where would she go with three kids? She told me that once she had convinced him to stay in a facility that treated alcoholics. After she saw him suffering through the detox period, she brought him home."

"He is a nonviolent addict. I never even heard them arguing. Besides, he is very smart. When sober, he goes to the library and reads history books. He is a veteran and served in Italy, fell in love with the country. PJ told me that he often talks about the Italian food. It's a shame that alcohol prevents him from fully using his intellect. He has so much potential."

"You are right. Eddie is a good man with an addiction that he cannot shed. It is such a destructive disease."

Earth Day

Saturday, April 22, I received via WhatsApp a photo of my twelve-year-old grandson, Luka, standing alone on a large grass covered space with a long metal-looking object in his right hand. The caption below the picture said: Luka cleaning his school grounds on Earth Day. His mother told me later that day that he woke up at his usual 7:00 am and demanded that she drive him to his school because he wanted to pick up garbage scattered on the playground. He told her, "It's Earth Day! We have to clean the Earth!"

"Did all the students take part in that initiative?" I asked her.

"No, he alone insisted on doing it without telling his teachers about it."

Luka spent several hours throwing different wrapping and several plastic containers left after student lunches into a large garbage bag, and he also pulled out weeds when he spotted them. His initiative to safeguard his school's landscape from careless littering surpasses the simple assumption that what he did served only to make him feel good about himself. Instead, he thought that his classmates deserve a clean environment during their outdoor recess. I am not sure if his teachers found out about his good deed and his understanding of Earth Day, but if they did, they could use it as a teaching lesson for other students of how each of them could contribute to preserve the bounty of nature's splendor around us. Luka's awareness of the importance of that day and his decision that he should take an active stance in preserving Mother Earth amazed me.

In the last several years, he has shown a special interest in plants, shrubs, and trees growing in both his and my front and backyard. He helps his mother weed and plant flowers, herbs, and tomatoes in late spring when the Michigan weather finally reaches temperatures required for growing, and there is no longer the danger of an unexpected frost. In addition to being our family's youngest environmentalist, his latest agronomist's prowess includes growing potatoes and carrots. In that, he follows in the footsteps of his great-grandfather, an agricultural engineer who specialized in different grains, his father's cousin, a forestry engineer, and the daughter of his father's second cousin, graduating with a degree in the pathology of plants.

I see my grandson as the hope for a future filled with clean air, unpolluted waters, and flora and fauna in abundance. He belongs to a generation that comprehends what the Earth needs better than those of us who preceded them. The world longs for leaders with a vision of our globe that doesn't rush toward self-destruction simply because no one wants to spend one Saturday morning cleaning his or her school's playground.

Boys 11 and up, 50m Breast, Heat 1

My son, daughter-in-law and I entered the bleachers of an Olympic size pool looking for empty seats. The humid, stifling air reeked of chlorine. Different age and gender swimmers circled the pool looking for their teammates and coaches. The chaotic scene lasted until their coaches directed them to the warmup area of the pool. The playing of the national anthem silenced the buzzing noise of the crowd and signaled the beginning of the competition.

"Do you see Luka?" I asked my daughter-in-law.

"Not yet. I wonder if he has found his team?"

"There he is, standing with his coach and the other Rays," I pointed him out to his mother.

"He is not wearing his team's red swimming cap. I hope his coach will help him put it on because without it we will not recognize him in the water."

Luka's race was scheduled third. I watched him patiently waiting for his turn. When the first group of eight swimmers dived into the pool, the bleachers erupted with screaming cheers. I was certain that the three of us would not follow suit because it would be out of character. Besides, Luka had been training with the Rays only a few months, thus we only expected that he would complete his heat. We also thought that his noncompetitive nature was a hindrance in this competition.

The whistle announced his race. Luka stepped on podium number six wearing his cap. I looked at his lean body with long limbs and wondered if he would have enough strength to swim two laps. Not knowing how to dive, he plummeted into the water and emerged at the same spot he went in. The other swimmers who dived were already several feet ahead of him. As he turned to begin his second lap, he suddenly lifted his head out of the water, as if looking to see who was ahead of him.

"He is swimming faster! He doesn't want to be the last one!" My son got up visibly excited.

"Go Luka, go!" My daughter-in-law and I sprang from our seats and loudly cheered him.

We took a photo from the scoreboard showing Luka's sixth place. He outswam two older swimmers.

"I am happy with how I swam today!" he said with a smile after coming out of the locker room.

That was all it mattered that day.

Chasing Yellow Butterfly

The winter of 2021 was almost over when I decided to go for an early walk. The last snow melted exposing rotting leaves laid next to the asphalted path. The temperature was in low digits but above freezing. I put on my fleece lined windbreaker, thick tights, earmuffs, and woolen gloves. Halfway through my route, I noticed that my usual mask-less elderly strollers, my contemporaries, were missing. I attributed that to their waiting for the afternoon sun that the forecast had predicted. Instead of my habitual focus on the rapid pace I try to keep, I slowed my gait and observed the surroundings. Suddenly, I noticed a slight commotion on the thin layer of leaves on my right. Out of it sprang a small bright yellow butterfly that proceeded to fly in front of me. I sped up my pace that became a run because I wanted to reach my unexpected companion. I had no intention of capturing it, just to follow it, and enjoy its fluttering in the air. I felt that wherever the butterfly took me there would be a new beginning waiting for me. He was a messenger of hope, that phoenix is still possible. My chase ended when the butterfly soared above my head and disappeared into the woods on my left. I resumed my walk at a slower pace and smiled as if trying to make the whole world smile with me.

Lifeless

My daily four-mile walk on Burton Street is usually uneventful. Dressed according to the outside temperature, I observe the changing of the seasons by looking at the trees on both sides of the road. In winter, I can see the frozen pond on my left and the smaller lake on my right because the lush green of the oak and maple trees doesn't obstruct my view. Occasionally, I cross paths with dog walkers, an Asian couple carrying two-pound weights in each hand, a chubby, slow-walking young woman with earplugs, bicyclists warning me to move further left or right on the cemented sidewalk in order to breeze by me unobstructed, and three chatty middle-aged girlfriends.

Last week I saw two motionless deer lying next to each other on the grass near the road. I didn't cross to the other side to verify if they were alive, but having found them in the same position on my way back, it confirmed my suspicion that they were killed by a passing car. I couldn't see any blood around them, just their white furry bellies sticking in the air. The whole scene disturbed me because their dead bodies made me think how an idyllic landscape can turn into a tragic one in a matter of seconds, just as a person's life can be changed unexpectedly by a single, seemingly impossible event. I thought of a friend of mine whose car was struck from behind by a speeding Honda. He was listening to NPR while waiting for the green light when a distracted driver rammed into his Toyota. The impact of the blow rendered him unconscious, and EMS transported him to a nearby hospital. His car was totaled, but he survived by a stroke of luck.

The deer were not as fortunate. I imagined them crossing the road in the dark and blinded by an automobile's headlights, they froze in the middle of one lane unable to run to the other side. Deer sightings in different neighborhoods have become quite common in the last decade due to the overbuilt new subdivisions, thus restricting natural areas where they and other wild animals used to live. Human beings have taken possession of their natural habitat and by doing that have endangered their existence.

A week passed after my first encounter with the dead deer when I walked by another lifeless one just a foot away from me. The impact must have been powerful because it launched the animal several feet in the air and over the grassy ditch to the extreme left of the sidewalk. My stomach turned in horror when I saw at the fresh blood seeping from the deer's mouth. Its dark eyes were open staring straight at me, as if wanting to let me know that it was too young to die. Indeed, it was just a fawn. Having been the youngest in the herd, I imagined it lagging behind its mother and siblings while they were crossing Burton.

On my next day walk I noticed that someone had moved the fawn's body. I'll never know if one of the neighbors had done it or the city has a special service for removing animals killed by passing vehicles. I decided to drive below the speed limit day and night to give myself time to stop before the furry crossovers. They deserve to live their natural life, just as we humans should honor ours to the very end.

When a Gun Pops

License and registration, sir! – Pop – Officer Down. Squealing wheels of a fleeing car.

The State of Grace

The other day, waiting at the Meijer checkout line, I heard a woman standing in front of me telling something in a hush voice to her teenage daughter. I was only able to grasp the word "grace." That word made me think about its meaning. I knew that there were multiple interpretations of it, from biblical to secular, but I wanted to define my own understanding of it. I thought of church-going friends, of the Bible study people I have met, and of acquaintances that always said grace before each meal. I concluded that none of them fit my definition of grace. They were all kind, generous, and full of empathy for those who suffered physically and mentally. They were the embodiment of Christian values, and yet underneath their charitable undertakings lay only one emotion – feeling good about oneself, a self-affirmation through appropriation of grace as a guiding principle.

I have witnessed only twice in my life the act of divine grace performed by two non-practicing Catholics—my father and my husband. The two events took place decades apart. After having broken her hip, my maternal grandmother, Anastazija, stayed with one of my aunts who lived on a farm. Her children decided that she would get better care being with their sister than in a nursing home. My parents and I lived in the city and would visit her every other weekend.

It was an early spring Sunday, still cold with nights in subzero temperatures, when my mother asked my father to drive us to her sister's farm. I was in middle school and would have preferred to spend the afternoon with my friends, but my parents insisted that I come along. I remember the three of us entering my grandmother's frigid bedroom with the small fogged up windows, and the heater shut off. When she saw us, she smiled from her double bed.

"I am glad to see you!"

"Mama, it is cold in here. I'll turn on the heater. Aren't you cold?"

"Eve turns it off when she goes shopping," she said matter-of-factly as if approving her daughter's rational that the electricity bills were too high.

My mother looked at my dad and me still standing by the door and said:

"The room reeks of urine and feces. Eve should change her diapers more frequently and wash her."

Upon hearing that, my father neared his mother-in-law's bed, slowly uncovered her, and looked for a second at her soiled nightgown and the bottom sheet under her soaked from the leaked diaper.

"Bring a bucket with warm water and old towels. We have to wash her," he ordered to my mother.

I watched the following scene unfold in front of me. While my mother was looking for items that he asked for, he was carefully taking off my grandmother's nightgown, telling her softly that the room would be warm soon and that they would heat up a bowl of chicken soup for her. When my mother showed up with the bucket and the soap, I anticipated that she would clean my grandmother. Instead, my father proceeded to remove the feces and gently washed her bottom. My grandmother didn't object to his intrusion into the most intimate part of her body because she understood that it came from the depth of his humanity. He dressed her in a clean flannel nightgown and tucked the down comforter around her.

"Thank you, Joseph! I feel much better now," she said while her eyes glistened with tears.

That Sunday afternoon, my father demonstrated the true meaning of grace. He did something that not even my mother expected him to do. He didn't need praise for helping his mother-in-law, nor did he expect a favor in return because his grace lifted him above the ordinary.

Years later, my husband bestowed on him the same grace when he was hospitalized for a urinary infection. At that time, my dad was ninety years old, walked with a cane after his second hip replacement surgery, and suffered from ailments typical of a person of his age. My husband and I drove to the hospital on his release day. While I was packing his clothes and hygiene items, my husband helped him to the bathroom as he requested. He couldn't take off his pants and underwear quickly enough and defecated on himself. Instead of calling the nurse aide or me to wash him, my husband only asked me to hand him my dad's clean underwear and trousers. Only after dropping off my dad at his house, did he tell me about the bathroom incident but without going into details because they didn't matter to him. I, like my mother decades ago, didn't expect such a kind gesture from my husband. He was just a son-in-law who was supposed to drive him home, and not a caregiver; it was my duty to help him. And yet his compassion preceded mine and led him to the grace that my modest father never saw as a repayment of his many moons ago.

The Kidney

"Harry, did you hear that Kevin's wife died?" Monica asked her husband while reading the obituary page in their daily.

"No. When did it happen?"

"Three days ago, according to the obituary."

"Does it say what did she died from? She was only fifty if I remember correctly."

"Yes, after a lengthy illness. Kevin was not specific in his announcement which one, but I recall my last conversation with her when she mentioned the dialysis that she was receiving three times weekly. I don't know what was wrong with her kidneys, but they obviously stopped working. The first time I heard about it was from an instructor I had met at a pedagogical seminar years ago. The woman knew her from another conference and told me that she was a diabetic and undergoing dialysis."

Monica recalled meeting Kevin's wife, Ada, at one of the Fourth of July picnics that Harry's automobile parts company used to organize for its employees. She was a tall, broad-shouldered woman in her thirties who always wore simple solid navy- or maroon-colored button-down dresses. Her hair was naturally ash brown and framed her makeup-free roundish face. She used to bow her head and lean forward when talking to other women because she towered over them. By assuming that pose she wanted to appear shorter and create an intimate distance for a cordial chat. She taught science in one of the Dearborn public schools. Monica liked to talk to her about their classroom experiences despite having taught a different subject; hers was English. She found Ada to be a more interesting collocutor than other wives whose usual topic of conversation was children and their activities. She talked in a calm, straightforward manner as if explaining a novel math concept to one of her students, but Monica didn't see it as patronizing because she often tended to communicate with others the same way herself. She called that a "professional deformation."

At the subsequent company picnics Monica noticed Ada getting skinnier and paler. She also watched Kevin's considerate behavior toward his wife. He would bring her a plate brimming with vegetables, slices of bread, and a glass of ice water. He would cover her back with a throw when the evening chill sneaked into the picnic area. His tentativeness and love were obvious.

"We must go to the wake. When is it?" Harry insisted.

"At 5:00 on Friday."

When they entered The Voran Funeral Home's viewing room, they found it full of people who came to express their condolences to Kevin, their three children, and the rest of the family. They were company employees, Ada's colleagues from work, friends, and neighbors who gathered in small groups and exchanged memories of her. Kevin was composed and gracious while mingling among them and thanking each person for coming. Monica noticed that he wore a gray suit instead of black, the customary color for such occasions. On the other hand, she remembered a neighbor, whose husband killed himself, dressed in a bright red dress during the visitation. That made her think about colors and their different symbolic meanings in Western and Eastern cultures that she had read about some time ago: white in the West stands for purity, peace, virginity, and the list go on, while in Eastern countries it symbolizes bad luck and mourning. Consequently, in India widows wear white. Westerners associate red with strong emotions ranging from positive such as love and strength to negative like anger and revenge. The Chinese call it a "lucky color" because it brings energy, prosperity, and health. Their brides tend to wear red wedding gowns. Black is the most complex color because its symbolism changes not only across diverse cultures but also within the same one. As an example, for Westerners it signifies mourning and sadness, but it is also associated with rebellion and youth. In China, it means immortality, stability, and power. Gray, considered a neutral color, comes in different shades that determine their symbolism ranging from positive to negative. Monica understood why Kevin decided to wear the gray suit. It perfectly represented who he was—a stable, balanced man whose life was in transition and required calmness for the sake of their children.

While her husband was chatting with his work associates, Monica joined a group of women that she knew from their summer picnics.

"I don't know how Kevin is going to manage work, kids, and the house," one of them expressed her concern.

"Perhaps he has family in the area that can help him?" Monica suggested.

"Well, he could have avoided the situation he is in now," another woman chimed in with an accusatory tone of voice.

The group looked at her puzzled and eager to know what she meant.

"I heard that he was a perfect match for giving Ada his kidney, but he refused to do it."

"It might be just gossip." Monica tried to lessen the impact the woman's revelation had on everyone.

"No, it is true. I heard it from a nurse present when he declined to sign the organ donor papers."

Monica decided to move to Harry's group to avoid listening to further comments on the subject. Soon after, Kevin joined them. She looked at him and his gray suit with different eyes, especially when he began to talk about his plans to buy a new car. He never mentioned Ada, as if she had never existed.

Perhaps his lighthearted behavior among friends is his mechanism for processing his grief, Monica thought for a second, but the fact that he declined to save his wife's life she considered the ultimate act of selfishness at the level of a sin. To her, his grayness stood for death.

Before leaving the funeral home, Monica glanced one more time at Ada's body in the casket. Her face was serene and peaceful as she was in life. There were no traces of her prolonged, health-related suffering nor blame for her husband's betrayal. As if she understood that, underneath his steely appearance, was a weak man that she led by the hand through their marriage. She forgave him because her love for him and her family made her strong enough to be able to overcome his weaknesses.

In the car Monica couldn't resist asking her husband: "If I needed an organ transplant and you would be a perfect match for it, would you give it to me?"

"What kind of stupid question is this? Of course, I would give it to you!" he quickly replied, sounding almost offended by my question.

She was satisfied with his answer but decided not to tell him what prompted her to ask him. She didn't want him to think less of Kevin, his good friend. She also didn't let him know that her renewed driver's license didn't have an organ donor symbol on it. The reason for opting not to add her name to the registry was self-justifying—the list of organs for donation also included the corneas, which she was not willing to give because she believed that this would disable her to see, guide, and protect her children from above. To abandon them would be an unconscionable outcome of her passing.

Greed

In Christian teachings greed is one of the seven sins. As a non-church-going Catholic, except for the observance of Christmas and Easter, I find this sin especially offensive because I see it as the cause of both individual and world descent into immorality and irrationality. I recognize the multiple faces of greed. On a grand scale there are countries whose social and political ideologies motivate them to seek global dominance. Individual avarice, on the other hand, creates a cheap person. I have met several of the latter. Often, they are people with a high income who manage their money with the outmost care, which in its essence would not be a negative character trait. Unfortunately, many of them become stingy with others outside of their narrow family circle. I find their behavior extremely irritating because they successfully wiggle out of situations in which they could easily be generous but opt to hold on to their wallets. I tend to compare them to those who are generous despite living on modest earnings, which highlights their greed even more. In regard to avarice, I categorize people in two groups—givers and takers—because the actions of both groups are determined by their attitude toward material goods. The following examples illustrate my point.

I hadn't seen my friend Marcia for several months, and we decided to meet at Panera for breakfast. She is a handsome, average height and weight, gray-haired woman in her early sixties, working full time and living in a small bungalow on the outskirts of Detroit. Divorced since her children were teenagers, she wasn't interested in dating. Her ex-husband never paid alimony, and she had to work multiple jobs to support her family. Her two sons and a daughter are married now and live in different states. After her divorce was final, we celebrated it with dinner at Red Lobster. I insisted on paying the bill, and she reluctantly allowed me. In subsequent years, whenever we met for breakfast in different restaurants, I would rush to yank the bill from the server, not giving her time to put her credit card on the table. She would heartily object, but I knew that the money she was making barely covered her monthly expenses for food, gas, and utilities. It was the right thing to do, especially because I could afford it by living in a two-person income household.

We both exited our cars at the same time and hugged.

"Hello, Marcia, I am so happy to see you! It has been too long!"

"Indeed, we should not postpone getting together for half a year!"

We sat at the booth, close to each other to be able to talk about our lives and gossip without being heard.

"How are the kids? And the baby?"

"They are all doing well. He is walking, but his grandparents continue to carry him around when they visit."

"Wait a few months, he himself will tell them no."

We ordered Western omelets and coffee and chatted for two hours. The waitress was giving us dirty looks because there were others waiting at the entrance to be seated. Marcia finally said:

"I think that we should leave because they might throw us out. "

She waved to our server.

 "Could you bring the bill, please."

I opened my purse to take out my wallet, but Marcia moved my hand away.

"I'll pay. Today is my turn. You paid the last time!"

"Let me at least leave the tip."

"No!" she said decisively while the waitress was nearing with the bill in hand.

With the kids out of the house, and having gotten a promotion recently, Marcia suggested that we take turns paying for our breakfasts and the occasional cocktails in the afternoon. I agreed because I knew that she was proud to be able to treat me and her other friends. By working as a head administrator, she could also afford the remodeling of her bungalow. She hired a neighborhood builder to retile the bathroom and paint all the rooms in antique white. Marcia also donates yearly to causes she believes in and to her church. Furthermore, she helps take care of her elderly parents, gladly watches her friends' pets when they are on vacation, organizes parties, and lends a hand to those that are moving. Marcia exemplifies Webster's definition of a true giver.

Two other friends of mine are also greedless. They value money not as a signifier of their social prestige, but as a means of a comfortable living and being able to share it. For example, my friend Chiara and I continue to argue about whose turn it is to pay for our weekly coffee klatch at Starbucks. We both insist on doing it. Tammy, another friend of ours, watches our house, waters the house plants, and pays any unexpected bill that arrives while we are traveling. She also forbids me to pay for her Carmel Macchiato at a nearby Lantern. To reciprocate for her kindness, I like to buy her cotton, long-sleeve tops that she wears year-round. She hates shopping; thus, my tokens of gratitude are always welcome.

However, I know a few penny pinchers that are unaware of being such. Those are people who see themselves as superior and perfect in the way they live their lives and interact with those outside of their orbit. They are high earners who seldom take time off from their work, and when they do, they limit themselves to one-week increments. They are workaholics, not because they love their job but because they love the money that it generates. One of those people is my cousin, Ed, a CEO in a large company that produces automobile parts for foreign made cars. He lives with his wife, Ruth, and their three girls in a six thousand-square-foot home in a gated Bloomfield Hills subdivision, drives a Porsche, Ruth has an Audi, and the girls attend the Detroit Country Day K-12 school. They recently remodeled their mansion and spent hundreds of thousands of dollars on top-of-the-line kitchen appliances, bathroom fixtures, mirrors, and the list goes on. They buy brand name clothes for their children and themselves, pay for their different after-school activities, often order food when Ruth doesn't feel like cooking, and eat out at both well-established and newly opened restaurants. Those are the perks of Ed's job.

The reverse side of their coin's head is the fact that Ed has only two friends that live in other states, and the same is true for Ruth. They talk to them sporadically, mostly returning their calls. They only entertain the family when celebrating birthdays and religious and national holidays every other year, and then they ask others to bring a dish or two as their contribution to the meal. When we attend those parties, I always bring either an appetizer, a side dish, or a dessert. Their excuse for not having more gatherings with others in their beautiful home is that their weekend schedule is for completing tasks they are unable to do during the week.

A couple of weeks ago, I invited Ed and his family to dinner since we have not seen them for a while. When I opened the door, I saw Ruth grinning and holding an unwrapped bottle. While handing it to me, instead of the usual greetings and hugs she said:

"We went to a wine tasting last Saturday and bought this Cabernet that we liked a lot for you. It was among the most expensive wines on the list. Let's not drink it now and save it for a special occasion."

She was just short of telling us its price, but I found it out on the Internet the next day–$40– pricey indeed. After Ruth's self-affirming generosity in bringing such an expensive wine, I decided to open a bottle of Grgich Hill's Cabernet Sauvignon but without mentioning its $70 price. My husband and I are recent retirees, comfortable with our monthly income coming from the SC and our private pensions, but we were never in Ed's earning bracket. The wine I opened was a birthday gift from one of our generous friends.

Throughout the years, I followed Ed and Ruth's behavior in restaurants that we attended with the rest of the family, and two or three times with them alone. They always suggested splitting the bill, but if one of us offered to cover it, they never objected. I witnessed them paying for pizzas if there were just a few of us. Their Christmas lists had expensive items on them that most of us couldn't afford, and I stopped asking for their gift suggestions. On the other hand, they had a budget for the amount they were ready to spend per person, and not every family member made the cut. For example, Ruth excluded her siblings. I sometimes wonder why Ed turned out to be such a miser. He grew up in a middle-class family, lacking nothing because my aunt and her husband both worked. There was money for vacations, tennis lessons, and soccer camps. Ruth, on the other hand, grew up in a one-income household, and the money was tight, but once she got her hands on it, instead of spreading it around, she deemed it sufficient to spend it on Ed, the children, and herself, donating to their church, and to one more charity of their choice that would showcase them to the community as true philanthropists. Unfortunately, their donation failed to improve their image of being cheap because people had already figured them out after seeing their behavior in various social situations.

Generally speaking, I find it to be in a poor taste when hosts mention how much the crown roast beef cost after someone compliments the tenderness and flavor of the meat.

"It should be good considering how expensive it was."

That was the usual answer of a couple who would occasionally invite us to dinner in their house. We met them at one of our friends' birthday parties. For some reason they liked us despite our opposing views on diverse subjects. We must have intrigued them by being different from their Country Club members, less polished and preppy, blunter and more emotional. They owned a stable of horses, took vacations in Europe, and drank only French cognac. In brief, they had plenty of money both inherited and earned.

An appropriate reply to the praise of the crown roast beef would have been just a simple, "Thank you!" or "I am glad you like it!" followed by a humble smile.

I am always amazed watching those who have perfected their tricks to get themselves out of paying for their meal. An acquaintance of mine used to order the most expensive items on the menu and would disappear in the bathroom when one of the guests sitting at the table would call the server to bring the bill. She would return to the table after fifteen minutes when she was sure that others had paid for her dinner. She was well off after her husband died and left her a house, an apartment in Florida, and all his investments and savings.

Another acquaintance used to suggest that we split the hamburger and the salad because she would not be able to eat the full order by herself. One look at her was sufficient proof that that she was able to munch not one but two hamburgers. She was a tall, one-hundred-and-ninety-pound woman who hid her nonexistent waistline with wide, demure-colored tunics. I never agreed to her suggestion and watched her devouring her lunch in a matter of minutes while I was still trying to finish the remaining half of mine. Was she cheap or on a diet? I wondered. I tend to believe in the former because her corpulent stature remained the same for years.

An additional example of ingrained greed was my childhood friend Laura. At work she was known to ask other smokers for a cigarette, claiming that she forgot her pack at home. She was a chain smoker for years; thus, no one believed her. They were certain that she had an unopened pack of Marlboros in her purse. One of her coworkers whom she would ask daily for a cigarette decided to quit smoking.

"Besides breathing better since I stopped puffing away, what really makes me happy is the fact that I no longer have to give my cigarettes to Laura!" she said victoriously to her other colleagues upon entering the office one morning.

Cigarettes were not the only thing that placed Laura into the category of those who use others. One July she invited a group of us girlfriends to celebrate her birthday in a well-known ice cream and pastry shop. Each of us ordered a coffee and an ice cream. We brought her presents that she excitedly opened praising their colorful wrappings and contents. When the waitress handed her the bill, she coyly smiled and lifted her brows in surprise as if the woman erroneously expected her to pay. Laura assumed her usual ladylike demeanor of detachment from the present situation when the rest of us realized that she had no intention of covering the bill. The situation was awkward and embarrassing for everyone except for her.

"Girls, let me treat you today!" I said and gave the server my credit card.

"This was fun! We should do it again!" Laura cheerfully ended her birthday celebration, ignoring the custom that who invites others to his or her birthday outing treats.

I felt stupid and used afterword instead of being happy to spend an afternoon with my girlfriends. We all agreed to wish Laura a happy birthday via phone call or an email next year.

The aforementioned examples of generosity and greed altered my behavior toward people. Sometimes I regret not having remained the once naïve and trusting person that only saw good in everyone. Others' actions and reactions taught me to be cautious and not let people take advantage of my gullible nature. Unfortunately, I still stumble into situations that I don't foresee as a set up for manipulating my original good intentions. Well, I have learned to live with it. Being a giver is much more awarding than existing as a greedy taker.

The Handwritten Letter

"**M**ark, did you bring in the mail?"

"Yes, it's on the counter in the kitchen. I have to go to Meijer to pick up my medicine. Do you need something?"

"Persimmons if they have them. I am getting tired of apples and grapes. Also pick up my sugar-free caramel coffee cream."

"OK, I'll be back soon."

Nora flicked through a handful of flyers offering services at a discount from furnace inspections and repairs to cremations when she came across a long white envelope addressed to her. She immediately recognized Maya's handwriting—small letters and dense word spacing. Eager to read its content, Nora tore open the envelope's flap and pulled out the neatly folded stationery.

"Dear Nora and Mark, how are you? When the children were in Pompano Beach at the same time as all of us were, time passed fast. I had to return home sooner than anticipated. Nora, do you remember our dances at the Golden Shell when we were fifteen? Our parents accompanied us. I still remember one dance with a local fisherman called Furbo. He had red hair like a fox's tail. He was good-natured, an orphan raised by his grandfather, also an angler. I think that his parents drowned on their way from Cuba to Miami when their flimsy, overcrowded boat sank. He and a couple of other passengers were rescued by a group of tourists on a yacht sailing nearby. Furbo and his friends didn't have money to buy tickets to enter the Golden Shell; thus, they sat on the low wall that circled the dance floor and watched us girls dancing with guys in creamy trousers and crisp white shirts. To my parents', my sister's, and my surprise Furbo suddenly jumped down from that wall and asked me to dance with him. My dad nodded in a sign of approval. Furbo wore light blue jeans, a striped blue and white T-shirt, and was barefoot. Dana was furious that I even got up to dance

with him, but my dad was so amused by the entire scene that his plastered smile lasted until our last turn on the dance floor."

In the remainder of the letter, she wrote about her oldest granddaughter, who was supposed to deliver any day, and about her son's breakup with the girl he was dating on and off for three years. That saddened her. She mentioned an interesting conference and a retirement party for one of her colleagues at the university, and was sorry for never learning how to drive, thus depending on her son for the transportation. She also described the Christmas decorations throughout the main streets in Lowell.

She ended the letter with a request and the final greeting:

"Please write to me but not in an email, just send a regular mail letter. This will be all for now, I love you both." Maya

Nora reread the letter and was struck by the fluency of thought, syntax accuracy, and precision of punctuation. It was the style of letter that her childhood friend used to write.

"I wonder why everyone thinks that there is something mentally wrong with her?" Nora asked herself.

People who knew Maya noticed that after becoming a widow, and shortly afterwards retired, she turned over all the daily house chores, the care of her health, and finances to her younger son, Dean, who lived in her house. She became a helpless dependent. Dean took her to a psychiatrist who diagnosed her as being in an initial phase of dementia.

When Nora met her in Pompano Beach, Florida, once a year, she behaved the same way as always. She expected that others would entertain her by asking her about her family, her past teaching career, about fashion, and her attendance of classical music concerts. She seldom inquired about their lives because she simply was not interested. If they volunteered information, she would patiently listen without commenting or posing further questions. Years before the psychiatrist's official diagnosis, her colleagues and friends thought there was something amiss with her flat emotional reactions, but they debunked that conclusion when she would perk up while ordering her usual drinks, a lemonade, or a glass of white wine. She also became animated when talking about her recent clothes purchases and a new hair salon she planned to visit. Nora concluded that Maya was egotistical and a taker with no regard for other people because she saw them as her underlings and servants. She dismissed the dementia diagnosis because it didn't manifest itself as it did with her mother, from the first onset of not being able to find her house after walking their dog, to the paranoia of being robbed by a cleaning lady, to the final stage of her illness when she no longer recognized her.

"Oh, great! You found persimmons! Was Meijer full? It took you a while."

"No, I had to wait to pick up Metformin. There was a line."

Nora knew that he was lying because she smelled the cigarette odor on his goatee and his clothes. Each time he went to Meijer, he would smoke one or two cigarettes standing by his car, a habit that he couldn't give up despite his cardiologist's warning that it could lead to another heart attack. He simply lacked the willpower to abide by his doctor's order. She stopped nagging him about it to avoid listening to his baseless defense.

"Are you crazy! I didn't smoke!"

"Maya wrote. It is a perfectly sane letter. Do you want me to read it to you?"

"No, just tell me the gist of it."

Mark hated long narratives and frequently told Nora that she talked too much.

"I am not going to summarize it for you. My point is that her letter is not the product of a feeble mind."

"I always knew that there was nothing wrong with her. She just likes to be catered to and doesn't really care about burdening her family. Her regal behavior or, better, her sense of entitlement never left her."

Nora found Mark's opinion a bit simplistic because it was hard for her to accept that her friend was a full-fledged user of others.

"There is something going on in that brain of hers that is hard to pinpoint because her actions and reactions are contradictory to the normal pattern of thinking," Nora tried to analyze Maya's state of mind.

In a conversation with their mutual friends, she compared the image of her brain to Maya's:

"Mine looks smooth like an avocado while Maya's is full of undeciphered convolutions." She concluded that her friend's present life was an enigma that only time would resolve.

Nora decided to type her a letter and send it via regular mail because her handwriting had become almost illegible after using a keyboard for years. Maya's, in contrast, remained a beautiful sample of old-fashioned lettering because she refused to learn how to use a computer. Her younger colleagues typed her scholarly articles since she convinced them they owed it to her.

The Painter

An anecdote about a famous Croatian painter circulated in the capital for several years. It was said that during his stay in a mental hospital he used to fasten his toothbrush to the end of a shoelace and drag it through the corridors. He saw his creation as a white, fluffy poodle that he named Yugo. His family committed him after he began to smear fresh paint over his acclaimed paintings displayed in multiple galleries of modern art. I find the painter's unhinged behavior highly creative, spirited and humorous, not destructive at all. I think that his goal was a form of self-reinventing through the process of altering his original work. In other words, his actions were an expression of his new self. They were not the outcome of his psyche's descent into madness. Instead, it is obvious that his soul soared toward a new palette of colors. According to me, he exemplified a reversal of one's earlier creativity into a novel artistic expression that society failed to recognize and labeled as insanity. I am sure that other patients in the hospital also live in realms incomprehensible to those outside of its walls - to the rational ones. For example, I don't understand why all publishing houses turned down my novel *Moby Dick*.

My Mother's Hand

My mother passed away at the age of 95 in 2011. She lived a year and a half before her death in St. Ana Nursing Home. My father decided to place her there because he could no longer tolerate her advanced dementia. The day he moved her was the last time he saw her. I continued to prod him to visit her, but he always had an excuse for not going. I stopped guessing what made him indifferent toward his wife of sixty-six years.

My father chose to remain in their apartment despite my suggestion to join my mother in the same retirement facility. As my father was increasingly unable to take care of himself, I hired a woman who prepared his meals, did his laundry, and cleaned the place. He seemed to be satisfied with this arrangement that lasted until he preceded my mother in death by seven months. Their passing in the same year made me sad, but my grief was short lasting. My friends would describe the loss of just one parent as unbearable. They would miss their mother or father for a long time after their demise and would frequently visit their graves. They also told me that their parents used to appear in their dreams, which made them happy. Not sharing the same feelings with them, I wondered what was wrong with me. I couldn't talk about it with anybody for fear of being judged as uncaring and emotionless.

Years later, one of my friends who lost her mother recently revealed the same detachment from the expected grief.

"At my mother's funeral I didn't even cry. I was sad but understood her passing as a transition into another form of existing."

Her explanation resonated with me. I realized that there were others struggling with the same feeling of apathy after the death of a parent.

"I felt the same way. Were you close to your mother?" I asked.

"Yes, we got along. How about you?"

"No. My mother and I never saw eye to eye. She was always critical of anything I did regardless of the success of my undertakings and would find something wrong in my pursuit of them. I decided not to entrust her with anything private and important to me."

"Briefly, she would get on your nerves, right?"

"Yes. With her dementia progressing we became even more estranged. She was not a bad mother, just overbearing and a know-it-all who expected me to obey her to the letter because she knew what was best for me. At times she was right, but mostly not."

"Do you ever dream about her? I still don't dream about mine."

"No, I never do because I fear that she would criticize me again. It would be more of a nightmare."

I didn't tell my friend that sometimes I feel my mother's presence while lying awake in bed at night. I feel her hand resting on the top of my head. It feels real, and I have never tried to touch it because I am terrified that by doing so, I would be tapping on a palpable object. The hand stays there for a few minutes as if waiting for something. By now I know what is expected. I tell my mother that I am fine, that the kids are okay, and I ask her to look after my dad. After that her hand disappears. I am sure that she visits me to make sure that I am healthy and safe even without her guidance. Her touch is a gentle pressure, a loving gesture that assures me that her love for me did transcend the great divide between us that once existed. I peacefully fall to sleep knowing that she will always protect me from above.

The Grave

Last summer, I was enjoying an afternoon on the beach. Just a few feet from the Adriatic Sea, I stretched out on my stomach on a thick towel to ease my discomfort lying on the smooth but hard cliff. The thick foliage of a fruitless pistachio tree shielded me from the burning sun. Near me, there were a couple of tourists reading and dozing on and off on their lounge chairs. The sea was calm and warm, and I frequently left my crossword puzzle unfinished in order to dive into the water. As I was getting ready for my third long stretched swim, my cell phone rang. My oldest cousin on my father's side, Lila, called me to let me know that the granite top on my grandparents' and parents' grave had moved an inch on the right, which exposed a bit of my mother's casket. Her voice sounded panicky while she was describing her horror when she saw what had happened. That cousin of mine is in her eighties, never married, and known for intentionally exaggerating the reality of different events. I listened patiently to her but took her story with a grain of salt. I am grateful that she visits this family grave regularly because I can only do it once a year when I am in town. On a narrow ledge under a tombstone is a small vase in which she puts artificial flowers and lights candles. After she had finished talking, I promised her that I would take care of the grave as soon as I returned to Zagreb.

I kept my word. The following day after my coming back from the vacation, I went to Mirogoj, the city's oldest cemetery, in which my paternal grandmother bought her burial site in the '60s. All her descendants have the right to a burial in it. It has graves of known Croatian writers, poets, artists, politicians, and several public figures, as well as common citizens. I like to walk along its paths lined on both sides with wild chestnuts trees. While strolling, I read inscriptions on tombstones. Some of them have only a name and a date of birth and death of the deceased; the others have a photograph and an epitaph. Graves that have fresh flowers and wreaths on them belong to people recently buried, while ivies and moss cover decades or even century-old ones, a clear sign that no one visits them any longer. Passing by those tombstones, I think about them as mementos of lives that meant something to somebody. Behind each name chiseled in the stone there is a story, and a memory safeguarded for posterity. Recently, I noticed headstones with nothing engraved on them. I find those morbid because it seems that their owner is waiting for someone in the family to die. A friend of mine told me that available burial grounds are scarce; thus, people buy them to make sure of having their resting place.

Mirogoj is usually a peaceful, meditative place until November, the Day of the Dead. Relatives come in hordes to honor and remember their deceased family members. They bring flowers and lit candles that make the cemetery explode with vibrant colors and lights. The custom is that after their visit, there is a festive lunch with the entire family. One of my friends takes care of multiple family graves and finds that day exhausting because of all the preparations involved in organizing it.

I took a cab to Mirogoj's entrance and then walked half a mile to my parents' resting place. The day was sunny, and I leisurely passed by a monument dedicated to a Fallen Soldier. I saw a large group of Asian tourists with their cameras ready because the cemetery has become a popular site to visit because of its history, architecture, sculptures, and its contribution to the country's national identity. It is listed in tour guides as a place not to be missed. After a few turns, first right then left, I walked up a slightly elevated pass to the row of several graves. My parents' is the last one, tucked in the corner underneath a tall cypress and flanked by overgrown evergreen hedges. I pay yearly for the trimming of those evergreens, but the cemetery maintenance crew is not too efficient in doing it.

I finally stood in front of the grave and saw that the granite cover had indeed moved by an inch toward the right side. I purposely didn't verify if my mother's casket was visible through the crack. I remember my friends laughing when I insinuated that my mother was probably sitting on that cover waiting for me. She never forgave me for moving to the States and, according to her, abandoning her. This is true. I fled from her because it became impossible for me to tolerate her infringement into my personal affairs. Yet, she remains an undeniable presence in my life. I often think about her and still blame her for mistakes I have made in the past. Now, as I am older, I realize that she passed on to me many of her character traits that I used to despise. For example, I am stubborn, driven, commanding, and outspoken when I should only be listening. I am grateful to have inherited her high-energy though. She worked full time, took care of my dad, the house, and me and experienced fatigue only in her late eighties.

Well, my mother was not waiting for me on top of that granite cover, nor did her hand stretch out to touch me through that crack. I looked at the names on the tombstone, at the years of their deaths, and suddenly became aware that I would be the next whose name would be underneath my parents.' I have already expressed my wish to my children to bring me back, cremated and in any container that will fit their suitcase, and place me in that grave. I want to return home, to the city where I was born and raised, to the country that knows my family name and to join my ancestors that had never left it. I owe this to them, to my children, grandchildren and all those who will come after me because I will leave them the family history without which they would lack a part of their identity to which they are entitled.

After a brief prayer and a short: "By, see you soon," I headed toward the cemetery's central office to make a claim about the vandalization of the grave. The woman in charge of the maintenance of the burial sites calmly explained to me that the granite top moved because the grout around it dissolved, which enabled the water and snow to gather around it and freeze in the winter, thus causing the shifting of the top. Her explanation sounded logical. I went to the shop of a stone maker who had covered the grave in granite years ago, and he told me that he would move the top to its original position. He also advised me to regrout every two years.

I called Lila to inform her that I took care of the grave. She said that she would inspect the work being done and let me know if there is still a problem. She insisted that the hedge needed trimming, but I left it to her to take care of it. What a shame, the crack was not wide enough to enable my mother to get out. She would already have been swinging an axe over the hedge's roots and not waiting for the cemetery crew to do it.

An Egg Under my Sheet

Summer, 8:00 am. I tossed aside the upper sheet and sat at the edge of my bed looking for my sleepers. I was fifteen years old. I noticed a bulge in the middle of the fitted sheet. When I lifted it, I saw a white egg lying on the mattress. I jumped onto my feet and panicked called out to my mother:

"Mama, come to the bedroom! There is an egg on my bed!"

She walked in, took one look, and calmly said:

"Somebody must have thrown it through the open window. Your bed directly faces it."

Her explanation didn't make any sense to me:

"But mama, I slept on that egg without breaking it!"

She glanced one more time at the egg and uttered:

"Bring it to the kitchen. I don't have time to talk about it now. Ilonka is visiting us and is waiting for me in the kitchen."

Ilonka was a Hungarian living in the States for many years but spoke English with such a heavy accent that it was hard to understand her. I remembered her as a short, rotund woman in her fifties that would offer homemade cookies made from the quince fruit to her guests.

"Perhaps she placed that egg in my bed, but why?" I wondered.

Fifty years later, I am still not sure if I dreamt of the entire event or if that darn egg really existed. Ilonka was real, but her visit was improbable because my mother had lost contact with her several years before the egg's appearance. I still cannot solve that mystery.

Panic Attack 1

The rainstorm began around two o'clock in the morning accompanied by loud thunder that sounded like it could topple the tall bell tower of the largest church in Rovinj. The tower's bells resound majestically on Sunday mornings before the first mass. The thunder woke me up, and I rushed to close the wooden shutters and prevent the rain from entering the bedroom. I love summer storms, the sound of raindrops, the look of wet, shiny cobblestones, and the fresh smell of the air after the rain stops. It excites me watching the night colors of the streets and the sea, listening to the rumbling noise descending from the sky, and anticipating the next morning that might surprise me with a wide blue sky without a single cloud floating across it. After the storm the sea seems motionless, and its surface is disturbed only by the landing of seagulls and the long dives of cormorants.

I woke up to a heavy gray day instead. My husband's depression grew in volume by the minute. He was verbal and described his anxiety as an inability to focus on anything else but himself and his self-inflicted mental torture. He didn't know a way out of it. One minute he was cold, the next one hot. I suggested having a coffee in a nearby bar and taking a walk. As soon as we sat at the small, round table at the bar, our friends joined us. Being surrounded by people whose company he once enjoyed, he became even more withdrawn. They didn't interest him. He looked as if he was ready to jump out of his own skin but lacked the energy to do it. After the coffee we took a walk on a path lined with tall cypresses on one side and the fragrant Mediterranean shrubs on the other. He continued to look at his cell phone that measured our strolling in steps, calories, and miles. He failed to connect to the beauty of nature around us because he thought that the numbers and charts that he was monitoring were the only real world. This walk after the rain was just one of my attempts to save him from ruminating.

I wondered what color the next day will bring- blue or gray? Will I be able to notice these colors or just put my sneakers on and count steps, calories, and miles?

Rovinj, Croatia, 7/24/2011

Panic Attack 2

Gray morning. The clouds did not lift as the forecast had predicted. I spent a sleepless night because I drank a cup of strong black tea earlier in the evening. I look at my watch on the nightstand; it shows nine o'clock. I am cold and trying to get warm under a lightweight summer blanket. My husband is awake in a twin bed across from mine and wants to know how the weather outside is. I don't want to talk about it because I was finally able to fall to sleep at daybreak, and my whole body feels heavy and achy. Suddenly he stretches his legs under the white top sheet and pulls himself to the edge of the bed. He sits there with his feet dangling, barely reaching the floor. His shoulders are slumped, and his head caved between them; his chin is low; his body language fills up the room with an uneasy anxiety.

"What's the matter?" I asked him, lifting my head from the pillow.

"I feel terrible. I don't know what to do. I am depressed, panicky; my blood pressure is higher than normal."

"Did you take all your medicines? Did you eat anything before?"

"I took them. I had some nuts and yogurt. I don't know what to do."

"Did you take a pill for your anxiety?"

"Yes, I did, but it takes one hour before it begins to work."

I am completely awake and heading to the bathroom. I wash my face and glance in the mirror at the dark circles under my eyes. I apply a small dab of concealer on them, add a few strokes of pink blush on my cheeks, a bit of lip gloss, and I quickly get dressed. I forget to brush my teeth and comb my hair.

"Let's have some coffee!" I say firmly, staying at the open door to the bedroom while he is still sitting on his bed.

This is not a suggestion; it is an order. I want him out of the apartment, in the open space, to feel the morning chill coming from the sea breeze that penetrates the bones, and to see other people.

We drank our first macchiato with a close friend, an architect, and talked about remodeling the apartment I inherited from my parents. The second macchiato is with two old friends. This friendship dates back to our teenage years, and my husband feels free to discuss his depression at length. They offer multiple mostly psychological solutions for it, claiming that they tried some of them out in the past and that they worked for them. We left the outdoor café after an hour. My husband's panic attack worsens.

"Let's take a walk to the church," I calmly suggest because I am afraid that he might refuse because it would be a steep climb over slippery cobblestones.

He accepts it. I am leading, walking carefully not to fall and trying not to bump into tourists that crowd the narrow streets because it is not a day for the beach. They are taking photos of century old houses and their gardens visible through their ornate iron fences. My husband checks on his cell phone the number of steps and miles he is taking. He becomes hungry and wants to buy a *burek* (a leafy meat pie popular in the Balkan Peninsula). I don't object to it in spite of knowing that the amount of fat and salt in it is not healthy for him. Food has always been my husband's comfort.

The afternoon brings peace. My husband is asleep, and I hope that his panic attack is, if not completely gone, at least diminished. Did I win or lose this time? I am not sure. The clock shows four thirty in the afternoon. It is time to start preparing dinner. I am sipping my second shot of brandy. The gray sky prevails.

Rovinj, Croatia, 7/25/2011

Panic Attack 3

I have had a panic attack only a few times in my life, on occasions that I don't recall specifically, but I remember the fast beating of my heart, butterflies in my stomach, and a sensation that I might burst and disperse into molecules - a terrible feeling of losing control of my mind and my body. This morning, I found my husband sitting slumped on the edge of his bed, staring motionless at the wall. His face was pale and sweaty, and his T-shirt was dotted with patches of perspiration that bled from his body to the fabric.

"I am having a panic attack," he said as a matter of fact.

I looked at him, not knowing what to say to break this cycle of his and my helplessness.

"I am going to the grocery store, and afterwards I'll wait for you at the café. I'll make your haircut appointment for today," I informed him in a calm, composed voice.

I left, empty headed, unemotional. I bought bread, a couple of yogurts and milk and sat at the café waiting for my husband to come. He arrived shortly after, joining me at the table, not saying a word. His perspiration continued. It was obvious that he couldn't control his panic. We drank our coffee in silence. He quickly browsed through the newspaper and wanted to go to the hairdresser since I was able to make an appointment. I accompanied him and waited while the middle-aged, redheaded stylist was cutting his hair and trimming his beard. She worked efficiently and fast being used to her male clients' impatience. She also poured me a cup of coffee because it is customary to offer a beverage to a waiting party.

While I was sipping my coffee, a one-armed man sitting on a bench next to me and waiting on his turn kept on asking me how my health was. Each time I answered: "Perfect." I had the feeling that if I had said anything else, this would have created an opening for him to tell me how he had lost his arm. I was not interested, did not want to partake in his life story. He paid no attention to my laconic replies, and he began to talk without a pause for breath about himself and other people only he knew. The teenager on the other end of the bench showed me the henna-drawn tattoo on her right ankle. The hairdresser was chatty and overly cheerful, often a sign of covering up one's private problems, while my husband was explaining to her why he was sweating profusely. He asked her for a paper towel to wipe off his face. I continued to drink my coffee and politely conversed with the other waiting clients, and yet I mentally removed myself from the entire scene. It felt like being in twilight.

On the way home while passing under a tall arch that leads to the old town, my husband spotted a friend of ours walking about fifty meters in front of us. He called his name, and the man turned around and greeted us with a broad smile. As always, my husband had nothing to say after the initial "Hi." He observed the usual, generic conversation between two people who have not seen each other for a while. Our friend told us news about his family and his cousin who suffers from advanced dementia and whom I have never met. I briefly informed him about the happenings in our family. This was an encounter that I would have preferred to avoid not because I was not interested in our friend's life, but because the events of that morning depleted all what was left of my empathy, patience, and tolerance. To cut this meeting short, I said that I was waiting for a phone call and needed to be home before noon.

As soon as we reached our apartment, I pulled down the shades in the bedroom and lay on my bed. I needed silence, dead air around me. All those people I met were chipping away pieces of me to fulfill their own need for comfort and commissary, and I could not give it anymore. After an hour of sleep, I woke up ready to listen to my husband's complaints about the weather and to his citations from Dr. Ornish's groundbreaking book about the reversal of cardiovascular disease the natural way by becoming a vegetarian. At least, this was what I understood while following my husband's monologue. At the end of it, I concluded that I have no desire to become a vegetarian, and if I live five years shorter because I love pork, I do not mind it. I still trust my good DNA and a healthy positive outlook on life to carry me through an acceptable existence without thinking about "power foods." It is my life after all. I should let my husband own his panic attacks and remove myself from that co-ownership.

Rovinj, Croatia, 8/1/2011

Yellow Tomatoes

It was 7:00 in the morning. On my way to Rovinj's open market, a small garbage truck was blocking one of the old town's narrow streets forcing me to squeeze between walls and its stinking open top full of trash-filled plastic bags. Its foul smell usually lingers in the air for an hour after the waste collectors finish their work. Their tossing of empty bottles and cans left from nearby restaurants wakes me up. That August morning was no different.

I got up quietly not to wake up my husband, quickly finished my morning routine in the bathroom and got dressed. I tried not to make noise descending the old wooden stairs and shut the entrance door as silently as I could. I love to go to the market while most of the city sleeps. It is small and covered with a green thermoplastic PVC roof, and it has ten rows of metal benches. That day the sky was blue, it was already hot, and another beach day was ahead. I reached the market in five minutes, and I found its counters half empty. Several vendors just arrived, unloading their fruit and vegetables, and displaying them neatly on their assigned benches. I know most of them because they are sons and grandsons of those that for years sold their products to my mother. I also buy my meat from my mother's trusted butcher Piero. I did not inherit any fishermen because my father was not fond of fish; thus, my mother seldom bought it. He had a hard time removing their fine bones and was afraid of choking on them. He only liked fried calamari that my mother preferred he ate in a restaurant because whenever she had fried them herself, the oil spattered over the entire stovetop. When I would visit, I insisted that she buy any kind of a healthy blue fish because I wanted to eat it baked with the skin and bones instead of the surgically cleaned fillets found in most American grocery stores.

I began to browse between benches and greeted vendors that knew me. I looked at their eggplants, at the green, red, and different colors and shapes of the peppers, Swiss chards, white, yellow, and red onions, lettuce, Romano and green beans, mushrooms, and fresh herbs and spices. Some vendors sell only seasonal fruit such as nectarines, peaches, plums, small pears, grapes, apples, and our favorite varieties of fresh figs. The explosion of colors and fruity fragrances revived all my senses. I was planning to buy red beefsteak tomatoes for a caprese salad when I spotted small pear-shaped yellow ones next to them. A robust older woman was selling them. I interrupted her as she was creating bouquets of lavender branches by asking:

"Are they sweet?"

"Try one," she replied without hesitating.

I had never eaten them before, and their sweetness surprised me. I bought half a kilogram. To my purchases I added Roman beans and a bottle of red wine from the man who sells it illegally to his trusted returning customers like me. He has a vineyard and makes a limited amount of wine with no additives or sulfates in it, the main reason why we like it. He hides it in the Coca-Cola bottles under his bench and places it into my large straw-made shopping bag quickly while I hand him the money.

Before returning home, I drank a cappuccino at an open café facing the sea and read several newspapers. The pattern I have been following for years. The waiters know me and bring my coffee, a glass of ice-cold water, and a cookie as soon as I sit down. We briefly chatted about the weather. When I bump into one of them after their working hours, we talk more about our personal lives. I never miss saying my goodbyes to them before leaving at the end of August.

My husband decided to join me on the beach in the afternoon. It was another lazy, uneventful day of swimming, reading the paper, and chatting with the two sisters who lay next to us. We all gathered under the widespread crown of a wild pistachio tree that protected us from the hot sun. We have known them for years. The younger, in her sixties and never married, is still attractive but tries to hide her age by wearing loud clothes and styling her blond hair in a way that the locks cover her forehead and part of her cheeks to make her wrinkles less visible. She is lively and temperamental, tells dirty jokes in a lady-like manner that always makes me laugh out loud, and is rude to those she does not like. She is the one who organizes their lives while they spend summers in their small studio in Rovinj. The rest of the year, the sisters live in their own apartments in Zagreb. The older one is in her seventies and a widow. She is more subdued and sophisticated than her sibling. She likes to talk about her husband, a successful executive, with whom she used to travel throughout Europe. A recent hip replacement hampers her walk over the uneven, rocky beach, which makes her look older than she is. The most entertaining thing about those sisters is their description of the meals that the younger one prepares. The following is a recount of one of their dinners:

"I made a bit of beef soup, a bit of lamb leg, a bit of roasted potatoes, and a tomato salad. I used only two large ones and a handful of small yellows."

Looking at the two of them sitting on their beach lounge chairs and eating with gusto salami sandwiches brought from home, followed by homemade cookies, one cannot but conclude that their idea of "a bit" is quite different from another people's understanding of it. Their large breasts and bodies that can barely fit into their one-piece bathing suits give them a zaftig appearance. They also like to sunbathe topless, which embarrasses my husband. I look forward to seeing them year after year because they belong to my beach inventory that does not undergo radical changes. The constancy of it all makes me happy and feel at ease.

We returned from the beach at six o'clock. Before putting my apron on, I poured myself a shot of *sljivovica*, brought from Zagreb. My parents used to drink "Vecchia Romagna" before lunch; therefore, I found an unopened bottle of Badel's plum brandy in their buffet. For dinner I prepared Swish chard, drizzled with the extra virgin olive oil and chopped garlic, and pan-fried sardines, and I placed the yellow tomatoes in a glass bowl in front of my husband's plate.

"Aren't they great?" I asked him as he bit into one of them.

"Yeah, but they don't have a... "

I forgot the name of a nutrient they lacked, according to him.

"They are not as healthy as the red tomatoes are. It's all in the red color," he explained in a patronizing tone of voice.

I stopped eating, was speechless for a few seconds, and then began to sob. Tears were falling on my plate, and I soaked my napkin wiping them off. My husband, stunned by my crying and not understanding what triggered it, asked me to stop, but I was unable to in spite of trying. Everyone has a breaking point, and the yellow tomatoes were mine.

After my husband's heart attack in May, he did not stop talking about the health benefits of certain foods that he was supposed to eat if he was to going to live. I learned more about nutrition than I ever wanted to know. He suddenly became aware that he had to give up what he had eaten in the past. For example, he used to fry eggs in butter and bacon, eat marbled steaks, and finish a loaf of bread in two days; he loved sweets, and his favorite fruit was bananas. All of these foods led to his obesity. In addition, he smoked two packs of Kents daily. After his early retirement, he spent most of his time lying on the couch, entertaining himself with the computer and watching TV. My eating habits are unlike his. I eat a lot of dairy products, all vegetables, and fruit. I also exercise several times a week, and I am a lifelong nonsmoker.

I cried because my husband's comment took away my pleasure of eating without thinking about why some foods are good for me and others are not.

"Next time, I'll buy only the red tomatoes," I said apologetically after composing myself.

I know that I will turn away from those tasty miniature yellow tomatoes in the future because they will always remind me of how fragile my happiness is, just seconds away from the deepest sadness and despair.

St. Lawrence's Night

It was August 12, 2011, St. Lawrence's Night in Rovinj, Croatia. The street lighting was extinguished, and torches lit the waterfront. Candles provided light in restaurants and cafes. I looked out of my kitchen window and noticed that an electric lantern hanging on the seven-hundred-year-old wall above one of the entrances to the city was indistinct as well. Crowds of scattered people were looking at the sky to spot shooting stars that are believed to be the tears that of St. Lawrence shed during his martyrdom. Music was blaring from the main square, and the lead singer sang the American evergreens that I love. There was a palpable excitement in the air. I soaked in the vibrant energy of life, the movement, the gaiety of the moment, and just for a moment, everything was all right.

Our friends left after we had finished the second bottle of red wine. We spent the evening sitting around the rectangular table in our small kitchen, laughing when recalling silly events in our lives, and we made plans to go by ferry to Venice next year. I forgot my husband's nagging, his negativism, and boredom, all of which are symptoms of his depression. What contributed to his despondency was a recommendation by his cardiologist to stop smoking after surviving a massive heart attack. After two packs a day of Kents during the last forty some years, the task in front of him was insurmountable. His personality changed radically, and I often felt as if I were married to another man whom I would not have agreed to wed four decades ago. I, as a nonsmoker, still have a tough time understanding the tobacco addiction, and I see it more as a hedonistic choice than as a disease. Should I be more tolerant of my husband's volatile moods? Perhaps, but this is his fight not mine. Throughout the years, I have altered my behavior to escape the cigarette stench: my coats are in a different closet from my husband's, I keep my purses in the laundry room, and I always shut my walk-in closet. At work, I exit the elevator if a smoker enters.

Prince's "Purple Rain" was echoing through my kitchen's open window. I wanted to dance to it, lose myself in the rhythm of the song, stop thinking, be close to somebody who breathes in unison with my heartbeat. My husband complained about the loud noise that I called music. We are two different people. There is nothing wrong with either of us; we just see life at a polar distance. What for him is an abyss, for me is a promise of a new height. Another song was soaring through the dimly lit town, romantic and young. There was going to be a better tomorrow.

Rovinj, 12/8/2011

Astrological Signs

I was born under the sign of Pisces. I cannot effectively explain to anyone nor to myself why I believe that the astrological signs hold the key to human relationships with nature and with other human beings. They are affected by the continuing rotations of planets, sun, moon, and stars that consequently cause mutable conditions in which each of twelve signs acts and reacts, thus it creates an unbreakable celestial bond between the cosmos and the sublunar world. I am certain that their floating nature has an impact on my physical and mental state. Therefore, I perceive astrology as the study of my soul, an arrow pointed to the future that could lead me to a greater awareness of being instead of just existing. I sometimes think that a friend who once a year follows the movements of my sign's celestial bodies knows my present better and foresees my future clearer than I could ever do. I feel that several of my closest friends also born under the same zodiac sign did not cross my path by chance, but rather by some higher metaphysical design.

Valentine's Day 2015

I woke up this morning to the sound of the wind that shook branches but could not sway the thick mist of large snowflakes on their way to the frozen ground. Through the large window of our bedroom, I watched them enveloping our backyard in whiteness. I wrapped my plush, pink robe tightly around me and slowly descended into our warm, semi-dark kitchen. After having opened all the blinds, I turned on the pot to heat the water for my first mug of instant coffee. Then I put on my puffer coat and booties on my bare feet to fetch the newspaper from our mailbox across the street. I have followed this routine every day since my retirement last December. I follow the same one I abided by when I worked. When I taught my first class at nine o'clock, I would get up at six thirty to be able to complete all the steps of my morning ritual. If for some reason I had to miss one of them, my whole day felt like something was amiss. The feeling of being dragged through someone else's routine disturbed me. I know how freakish and obsessive this sounds, but I function the best by following the order of my own design. However, I am able to dodge it pronto when presented with an interesting or exciting alternative, which does not happen often.

As I stepped on our circular driveway, I heard the opening of the entrance door behind me despite my having shut it. The strong wind had pushed it open. It also made the cold air feel even more frigid especially on my face and bare shins. I rushed back to the house, sinking my hands in pockets while carrying the newspaper under my armpit. The hot mug of coffee warmed my chilled hands. I read the *Walt Street Journal* for about one hour. I know that most of my colleagues and friends consider it politically incorrect to have a subscription for it because they find it overly conservative for their progressive views, but I ignore them. I am an open-minded reader and also subscribe to the *Detroit Free Press*, the *New York Times,* and *People Magazine.* I am interested to find out what people from all walks of life and backgrounds think because their thoughts deepen my understanding of them. Any political indoctrination borderlines with fanaticism and the idolization of its maker, and a leader creates masses of narrow-minded people and a country dominated by a single ideology. My retirement has freed me from an imposed narrative perpetuated by a government in power and enabled me to say what I think without worrying how others are going to interpret my words. Today's *WSJ* had interesting editorials on geopolitical affairs, an insert on the latest spring fashion, and interviews with several artists whose creativity is changing American popular culture. I learned new things about diverse subjects. If that labels me as being politically incorrect, so be it.

Having finished eating Greek yogurt for breakfast, I took a long, hot shower and put a red sweater on. I tried several times to wake up my husband to get ready for lunch in an Italian restaurant that we both like. I made a reservation weeks ago because the place booked early tables for Valentine's Day. He was asleep on the family room sofa lying with one leg bent, the other stretched out. This pose eliminates the painful cramps he has each morning. I looked at his face at peace, his head full of gray hair sunk into the cushion and listened to his rhythmic breathing accompanied by a light snore. After my last, by now irritated attempt, he finally opened his eyes and seemed annoyed by my interruption of his morning nap. It took him a few seconds to rise to a sitting position and several others to get up. He was silent upon returning dressed from the second floor where his walk-in closet is. While he was selecting which puffer jacket to wear, I was in the garage warming up my Honda for him not to sit in a cold car.

The unplowed street and the drifting snow made my driving difficult. My husband's mood improved, and he asked me:

"What is today's forecast?"

"Cold and snowy."

Valentine's Day has no meaning to him. He was surprised to see a crowded restaurant, and I told him what people were celebrating.

"Oh, I forgot."

It was just a statement, not an excuse or apology. He was eager to order his food to be able to return home as soon as possible and assume his lounging position on the couch. I enjoyed the veal Marsala and a glass of Chianti. Our conversation at the table focused on the food on our plates and nothing more. The snowfall intensified as I drove back.

A New Chapter

January 10. Today is the tenth day of my retirement. I taught my last class on December 14 and expected it to be an emotional experience considering that it marked the end of my forty-year teaching career. I felt indifferent, which meant that I was ready for a new chapter in my life. After having corrected the final exams and submitted my grades, I cleared up my office leaving boxes full of books and teaching materials in front of it. While driving back home on a boring twenty-five-mile-long road, I promised myself to keep a diary during that first year of not working. I wanted to record my feelings and thoughts that would accompany my decision-making processes as what to do with so much free time on my hands.

I broke my promise. Instead of writing the first entry into my diary on January first, I spent time saying goodbyes to my son and his family who drove back to Grand Rapids after having stayed with my husband and me the entire week. The mornings of all their departures were always hectic, not as much in reality as in my perception of them, and that January first was no exception. Our grandchildren slowed down their morning routine of getting dressed, eating breakfast, and brushing their teeth. They ignored their parents' nudging to hurry up. At the same time, I tried to act happy and chatted with them while our son was putting the luggage in the trunk. When I kissed their soft, pudgy little faces before they were strapped in their car seats, I sensed their compliance for the trip. As the garage door was slamming shut, I ran to the dining room window to see their faces one more time behind the semi tinted quarter glass of the SUV. The house became quiet and lifeless. While picking up the children's toys scattered across the floor, a deep sadness overwhelmed me.

It took me several hours to overcome that sinking feeling and motivate myself to begin packing for a four-day visit to our friends in Arizona. I was looking forward to seeing them knowing that they would ask me what I think about my new freedom. I didn't have an answer for them because I first had to reconnect with my inner self pushed aside for the longest time. The verb "must" was a leading driving force in my life, and my retirement enabled me to replace it with wonderfully hedonistic "want."

January 11. I went to bed late last night because I was watching an older movie, *The Departed.* I enjoyed seeing it the second time because of the unpredictability of the plot and the fine acting. Enigmatic people, ideas, and things have always attracted me since they challenge me to guess their true nature or what lies beneath their surface. My curiosity has often launched me toward that great unknown that never ceases to surprise me either with its steadfastness to never reveal itself or to suddenly become transparent. As I am writing this second entry in my diary, I realize how my "want" should come about. Since my teenage years, I have loved to write short prose pieces. I never showed them to anyone because I considered them solely as my entertainment. Following a hiatus of fifteen years, I went back to my writing and discovered the pleasure I once had drawn from doing it. I remembered and faced numerous ambiguous situations and people that inspired me to write about them.

The other day, I told our daughter how I planned to spend my retirement years; she encouraged me and suggested that we write something together. Her idea was that each Sunday one of us would choose the topic, and at the end of the week we would exchange our stories. The end result would be a two generational collection of short stories. I liked her idea. She was the first one to pick this week's topic — "Friendship." I am supposed to send her my story by January 18. Her title sounds more like a high school writing assignment, but I think that the thought behind it is personal to her. I hope that she will not stray into a flat-out confessional because that could diminish her broader understanding of diverse kinds and levels of friendships. I could be guilty of the same mistake. Well, we will see what we both come up with in one week's time.

I am going to Walgreens now to get a Retinol cream that is supposed to make the fine lines around my mouth less visible. Why do I still care how I look? I don't know, but I do. I suppose my goal is not to be seen as an imitation of my younger self, just improved and appropriate to my sixty-six years on this Earth.

I am not sure if keeping a diary is the best venue for my musings, but at least I will have tried.

The Retirement

Today is the tenth day of my retirement. In spite of having made a decision to keep a journal of my daily activities and musings during the first 365 days of my post-work years, I did not do it. The hustle and bustle that preceded Christmas pushed aside my original plan. January 1st was usually a day of saying goodbyes to my son and his family who live 120 miles west of my husband and me. Those mornings of their departure always seemed hectic to me, but to them they were just routine preparations before their ride home. Watching them packing their suitcases and passing by me as if I no longer existed, made me feel pushed aside and useless. Our grandchildren would notice their parents' hurried movements around the house not understanding that they needed to speed up getting dressed and eating their snacks. I was putting on a happy face and gently prodding them to do just that. When I kissed them before they entered the car, I could see that they were eagerly waiting to begin their return trip. As soon as I heard the garage door slam, I ran to the dining room window to take a last look at their faces through the backseat side windows. The house would fall silent, and its emptiness would overwhelm me with a deep sadness.

January 1st of 2015 was supposed to be a day that I could spend at my leisure. Our son and his family celebrated New Year's Eve with his wife's family, and my husband and I watched the ball dropping in Times Square at midnight alone. Instead, the day turned into a frenzy of making decisions about what to pack for my four-day stay in Arizona. I was looking forward to seeing our friends there and to celebrating my new freedom with them. I am not sure how I feel about being a recent retiree. Everyone keeps asking me about it, and I don't have an answer. I need more time to figure out how I want to use all those free hours on my hands. First, I have to stop quantifying time and let go of the verb "should." I need to pause, to think, and to reconnect with my inner self neglected for too long.

It is January 10. I can no longer retrieve days that I failed to write about in my journal. I guess that the part of my current existence unburdened from the grinding rhythm of everyday living, means that I no longer have to look back and remember things once deemed important. If my retirement is a synonym of freedom in the broadest sense, I can accept this.

Albums

Today's technology enables us not only to take high-definition photographs with our phones, but also to use them to create digital photo albums. In order not to lose them, we can store them on the iCloud or have them on a USB-Powered Photo Stick. The result of this technological progress brings us closer to the vanishing of classical leather-covered albums filled with plastic photo sleeves or magnetic self-stick pages. I see the practical advantage of computerizing our memories because they are better safeguarded than keeping them in the cumbersome, old-fashioned albums that could be difficult to save in case of a house emergency such as a fire. However, despite my better judgement, I still have fifteen leather-bound albums neatly stashed in a cabinet below a large bookcase in my study. The main reason for my attachment to them is the fact that I like to hold them in my hands, turn their pages brimming with photos that recorded my family's trips and festive occasions celebrated throughout the years. I saved all black and white pictures inherited after my parents' passing. Some of them are in their original slightly damaged crinkle blue paper-bound album, while the others are loose, and I keep them in photo storage boxes. They are populated with my maternal and paternal family members and me as a child and an adolescent.

Sometimes when I feel lonely and nostalgic, I pull out albums with decades old photos that my father took with his Kodak in my native Croatia. I look at familiar faces and remember the specific events that inspired him. My nostalgia instantly turns into a sense of belonging and owning my past that is an integral part of my present identity of being a Croatian American. I like to look at the photographs of my parents when they were young and at their wedding pictures. Among them is a black and white photo of my father and his friend standing on a sidewalk in downtown Zagreb. He must have been in his twenties, looking dashing and handsome in his wide leg pleated summer trousers and a polka dot patterned short-sleeved shirt unbuttoned below his neck. I am sure that his wardrobe reflects men's fashion in the forties because he remained a sharp dresser even in his later years. The picture also shows a leather-covered camera hanging on two straps on his chest. My father was an avid photographer, and that camera attests to his early interest in photography. His favored subjects were trees, domestic and zoo animals, and me. I hated the photos he took when I was a teenager because I always considered myself unphotogenic. I still believe that the camera doesn't like me even when I pose for a better take. I framed a close-up of a rooster that won him first prize in an art contest.

I am particularly fond of the photo featuring my mother and me during our summer vacation in the 1950s. It shows us sitting on a circular stone bench under a large tree with multiple trunks. I am still wearing my cotton bathing suit, and my straight hair is covering half of my face. My mother is clad in a white, puff-sleeved blouse and a midi skirt with large polka dots on it. Her hair brushed on one side and the fashionable sunglasses beautifully frame her high cheek bones. We are both smiling, she broadly and I shyly. Behind us is the Adriatic Sea and a group of middle-aged women in their one-piece bathing suits getting ready to leave the beach. It is a happy scene that I put in a gold frame and placed at eye level on a shelf on the bookcase in my study.

Those old albums still maintain their integrity of being faithful custodians of our past. They deserve to be cherished and protected because they are storytellers with a long-lasting memory. Technology's RAM is short lived because it is replaced in rapid succession by a newer version, thus leaving no time for that tender nostalgic moment.

Departures

Sunday evening, January 2004, face biting frigid wind relentless in its pursuit to punish those venturing out of their warm homes. Our daughter Mila flew back to Stanford to the temperate climate that she prefers over her native Michigan's winters. She usually stays with us for a week during her Christmas break. It was one of her departures that left me feeling sad beyond words. When I hugged her at the airport, I tried not to cry but there were times when I was unable to hold back, and my tears would slide down her neck and wet the collar of her puffer jacket. Seeing me cry would make her cry which would create a scene that her father, standing by his car and ready to leave after their brief exchanges of hugs, could never understand. According to him, Mila and I created an unnecessary drama in a public space, making him feel uncomfortable. I wish to be able to process my emotions the way he does in a logical and well-measured manner. Instead, I have to gather my entire mental strength not to give away what lies beneath the benevolent smile of mine.

When Mila moved to California to attend Stanford Law School two and a half years ago, I was proud of her achievement, and she was excited to go because SLS was her first choice. She drove with her boyfriend across the country in his black second-hand old jeep with a small U-Haul attached. I was abroad when the two of them loaded the jeep and the trailer, thus I can only imagine how they jampacked them with all their worldly possessions. They were heading toward new challenges and adventures unfathomable to them at that time.

As soon as we returned from the airport, I entered Mila's second-floor bedroom. It still smelled like her perfume, but her clothes usually scattered across the floor were gone and several damp towels lay by the tub in the bathroom, one of her habits that adds to her overall nonchalant attitude toward neatness. The emptiness of her room made me realize that a geographical distance between us could gradually alter our close relationship because I was no longer a daily feature in her life.

I questioned my place in it. Her phone call upon landing in San Francisco reassured me that I still matter.

After Mila's departure, I quietly settled into my routine of teaching, exercising, taking care of the house, and meeting friends and acquaintances. Mila and I talked weekly. During our last conversation, she told me about her visit in June. She wanted to surprise her father for his birthday. I was looking forward to seeing her and rescheduled all my appointments because I wanted us to spend time together. But her friends were in waiting as well. I didn't mind that she met them every evening as long as I could see her walking barefooted in her velour pajamas throughout the day and eating her cereal while reading the *Detroit Free Press*. We never missed going shopping at the mall and having lunch in "Charly's," our favorite fish restaurant. We would drink red wine and talk. She knows me well, and I didn't need to auto censor my thoughts, neither did she hers. We have remained firm features in each other's lives.

Four Snails

I stood in front of the mirror in our bathroom with room for only one person standing covered from the floor to the low ceiling with miniature, teal-colored tiles and observed a snail that I had placed on my forehead a minute earlier. He or she – I learned that snails are hermaphrodites – came out of its shell and was motionless for a few seconds as if making sure that no one would harm it. Then, the mollusk began to move slowly from my forehead to my temples and down to my cheeks, leaving behind a clear slimy track. I smiled because that slime was exactly what I needed. I gently removed the snail from my face and placed it in a transparent plastic container that I had perforated on the top and lined with lettuce. The walker joined the other three mollusks there. I noticed that one of them was hiding under the lettuce and was asleep. The other one attached himself/herself to the top of the container as if gasping for air, while the third one munched on the moist leaves. I put the snails' temporary habitat on the kitchen windowsill and headed to the bathroom to smear the slime all over my face. I decided to keep it on the entire evening while watching a movie on Netflix. My husband sat next to me on our old beige sofa that we agreed needed a replacement. He looked at me, with a smirk on his face, and asked:

"Who told you that snail slime can erase facial lines? Where did you find these snails?"

"Katrina, a friend of mine from high school, brought them to me this morning. She knows all about beauty treatments, especially about the proven benefits of snail slime. You should have seen her face, smooth as a baby's butt, and we are the same age. She has been using live snails for two years. Yesterday, when we met for coffee, she noticed the deep lines around my mouth. She suggested that I get rid of them because they make me look older."

"You are old! No matter what you put on your face, it is not going to smooth those creases. Besides, why do you care?"

His last question made me wonder why I really care about looking younger. I don't hide my age of seventy-three because I am still in good physical shape. I walk four miles daily and swim twice a week at a local YMCA and every day in the Adriatic Sea during July and August. Furthermore, I take Pilates classes and lift weights. I am never sick, but occasionally I pull muscles that takes longer to heal nowadays. I also follow the Mediterranean diet, and the results of my annual physical checkups satisfy my doctor. However, my face reveals my age, and that bothers me.

I guess that living in the era of striving to achieve eternal youth has rubbed off on me as it has on many other women of my age. Some of us continue to dye our hair thinking that silver strands would prematurely age us. I have been a redhead since my twenties and plan to remain as such. We wear clothes that are in fashion or those of us with a full figure tend to hide it under bright colored tunics that cover our protruding stomachs, the flab around our waistlines, and the cellulite-filled behinds that jiggle when we walk. We buy oversized glasses to hide the crow's feet and black circles under our eyes that concealer cannot camouflage. We still choose to wear blood-red lipstick despite the possibility that it can bleed into the fine lines around our lips, thus making them even more noticeable. When we were young, we cared about our appearances primarily to attract men, but as we age, we care more about soliciting compliments from our girlfriends when we meet casually for a coffee to chat about our daily lives as retirees and as grandmothers. We exchange experiences about using different day and night creams, serums with hyaluronic acid and Retinol, which brings me back to Katrina and her promotion of the use of snail slime to rejuvenate the skin.

After a hiatus of four decades, we reconnected in Rovinj, Croatia, five years ago. Both of us spend summers in that small touristy city, she as a director of classical music concerts and a mezzo-soprano performer and I as a vacationer and a frequent attendee of those concerts. The day she told me about snails, we met on the terrace of one of the city's oldest hotels situated in the main square across from the tower with a large clock that sometimes tells the correct time. We arrived simultaneously, which I appreciated, because as I am getting older, my tolerance for people's tardiness is waning.

Katrina is a tall, statuesque woman with a jet-black mane of curly hair that reaches her shoulders. Her full lips extended into a broad smile when she saw me, and I noticed her uncapped naturally white teeth. Aging has been kind to her. She has remained beautiful in her own way, as we say about those women who are growing older gracefully. She wore white pants, an attractive short-sleeved top with a flower design, and long dangling earrings. She seemed a bit heavier than the last time I saw her.

Before sitting down at the table, Katrina carefully selected a chair that enabled her to face me without turning her head. She explained that her neck was hurting her when she turned, but regular massages were helping to minimize that condition. She ordered cappuccino and proceeded to sweeten it with a packet of organic sugar that she took out of her white purse. Her motions were deliberate, while she was expressing her gladness that we finally had a chance to meet after being absent from Rovinj due to the Covid-19 travel restrictions of the past two years. Her demeanor mesmerized me because it fluctuated from sophisticated to the girlish giggle that I remember from our high school days. At that time, none of us knew that she had a beautiful singing voice. We only perceived her as being the most beautiful girl in class and a mediocre student. After graduation, she completed her studies of singing and performing German lied interpretations, which enabled her to have a successful career as a concert singer.

Suddenly, Katrina looked at my face intensely, asked me to turn from left to right to be able to thoroughly examine it as a cosmetologist would, and then said:

"Let's get rid of these lines around your chin and mouth."

"Well, easier said than done." I was about to tell her which creams I was using when she interrupted me.

"You need snails! Look at my face! I have been using them for two years. I'll bring four of them to you tomorrow."

"You must be kidding! What would I do with them? Where would I keep them?"

"I'll bring them in a plastic container with some lettuce in it. The important thing is to always keep the container wet and feed the snails every few days. Put several leaves of ivy at the bottom because they like to hide underneath them. You have to clean their new habitat regularly because they poop."

"It sounds like a lot of work, and, frankly, their slime disgusts me."

"Don't be silly. The slime is transparent, has no smell, and penetrates the skin in seconds. It becomes invisible. I sometimes keep it on my face the whole night, but you don't need to; several hours are enough."

True to her word, Katrina brought me four snails in a tiny plastic tub the next day. Not wanting to risk becoming the object of ridicule, I called two of my girlfriends and told them about the snails. Both found my story credible and went on a hunt for their own mollusks. The following months, the snails became the main topic of our daily conversations. One of my girlfriends found out on the Internet which food snails prefer. She told me that they love cucumbers. She recommended that I slice them very thin or grate them as she did because that way the snails could digest them without any problems. She also warned me not to give them bananas because after tasting them, they will refuse all other foods. The other girlfriend found out that it is important to let snails walk because they are gastropods, which means "stomach foot." They move by expanding and contracting muscles. In other words, they need their exercise for good digestion.

She went on to explain that she let her snails explore the cemented terrace behind her house while she watched the evening news. However, she soon realized that they should not be left alone to roam because one almost escaped into her garden by moving fast, which is contrary to the popular belief that snails are slow creatures. She caught the gastropod at the edge of the last step and decided to name him/her Speedy. I didn't name my snails but was able to identify them by their distinct personalities. One was lazy and seldom crawled out of his/her house;

the other would latch onto the side or the top of the container and remain there for hours; the shy one hid under the lettuce or ivy leaves; and the fat one was the most alert and would return to his/her shell only at night.

The three of us talked more about our snails' lives and their habits than about the results of applying their slime on our faces. Growing up, I never had a pet because my parents didn't like animals. In addition, we always lived in small apartments that could not accommodate any additional inhabitants. The four snails were my first pets, and I took exceptionally diligent care of them. I fed them lettuce and cucumbers and bought a larger plastic container to give them more space for moving around. I rinsed it and lined it with fresh ivy every other day. I let the snails crawl on my kitchen windowsill under my watchful eye to make sure that they didn't fall over the edge. Taking care of them felt like being in a Zen zone. I applied their slime on my face only eight or nine times during the two months that I had them because the beauty treatment they were supposed to foster became secondary to my pet experience.

I had to get rid of them because I traveled to Zagreb at the end of August. To make sure that they would have everything they needed for their survival, I found a grass-covered park surrounded by marjoram bushes that was watered daily and would provide shade. Those were the optimal conditions for my snails' happy existence after my departure.

"Was it hard for you to say goodbye?" the new owner of Speedy asked me.

"Yes, it was. What do you plan to do as a farewell for them?"

"I already bought a gigantic piece of lettuce that I will leave in a shady part of my backyard, where I will place all of them next Wednesday."

After my summer spent in the company of my snails, I no longer care about the creases around my mouth, and I will find four new mollusks as soon as I arrive in Rovinj next year. I already miss my slimy pets.

Ageless

My oldest cousin, Lila, never married and, still single, called me last September. We usually reconnect and visit at that time because she cannot stand the July to August heat.

"Is the clothes alteration place by you still open?" was her opening question.

"Yes, the woman works weekdays until 7:00 pm."

"I have a navy suit that my friend Magda gave me, but the skirt is too long. When can I bring it to get it shortened?"

"Whenever you want, but mornings are better for me if you want me to accompany you."

"Great! I'll take an Uber tomorrow morning."

Lila was punctual as usual, and we headed to the seamstress's shop. I watched her reaction when she entered the tiny room brimming with finished alterations hanging on one rack and the undone clothing on the other. On a table leaning against the back wall were stacks of colorful threads, scissors, pins, needles, and a measuring tape. The owner's small poodle greeted us with a loud bark and tried to climb up Lila's skirt. She quickly pushed it away with her foot, which visibly displeased the woman.

"What can I do for you?" she asked her coldly.

"I need my skirt to be shortened."

Lila's answer was equally frosty because she was taken aback by the seamstress's tone of voice and the messy ambience. She especially disliked the presence of her dog that continued to sniff her.

"You can change in the dressing room on your left."

Lila put on the skirt, and the woman suggested the length that would fit her height. My cousin is 5'1" tall, a bit heavier after the hip replacement surgery that makes her unable to keep up with her daily walks.

"This is too short! I want it three inches below my knees!" she issued her command.

I was surprised that the woman didn't throw her out at that point.

"As you wish," she replied, but the expression on her face signaled that she disagreed with Lila's choice.

I observed my cousin critically staring at her image in a large mirror and the seamstress pinning the hem of her skirt, and thought,

She is 86 years old, continues to pay attention to her appearance from her chestnut-colored died hair pulled in a ponytail on her nape to her Italian made loafers and London Fog raincoat in a classic beige tone. Her clothes' alterations, as well as the repairs of the handles on her old purses, confirm her belief that she still has more years ahead. Age has no meaning to her.

She reminded me of John, my neighbor across the street, a short man in his eighties who shares her life philosophy of living to the fullest until his final departure. After his wife died five years ago, the neighbors thought that he would sell their house and move to a retirement home. He surprised everyone by staying put. Moreover, last summer, I watched a landscape company clear his front yard of old bushes and overgrown perennials and replace them with small shrubbery and a blooming tree that would take years to reach its full height. In John's world he would see it happening. I also see him driving his truck and a red sedan each day, which means that he keeps up with his social life by visiting friends and family. On Easters, Thanksgivings, and Christmases I had noticed two automobiles parked in his driveway and people exiting them carrying platters covered with aluminum foil. He celebrates these traditional gatherings because he obviously believes that he owes it to life itself.

Lila and John are ageless. It's too bad that they live on different continents because they would understand each other perfectly.

The Contamination of a Family DNA

I have never been overly interested in genetic discoveries, not because I find them useless but because I see them as my personal regression into believing that our future well-being is sealed even before our conception. I pushed this ominous idea to the back of my mind, and it stayed there like an itch that I didn't want to scratch. However, after my mother told me about a slight pain in her right breast accompanied by a dark discharge from the nipple, I pressured her to have a mammogram. It was her first. The X-ray didn't detect any malignancy, and her doctor was unable to diagnose the cause of her symptoms that gradually ceased. I suddenly reversed my earlier indifferent take on genetics and concluded that a single faulty gene must have caused her problem. In the same year, my mammogram showed an impalpable small mass in my right breast. The biopsy result was a fibroadenoma, a benign growth. I concluded that those two health-related instances that we both experienced were not coincidental. The only logical explanation I reached was that my mother's gene traveled in utero from her into my blood stream and landed in my boob. I wondered if that was its only trip or if it had cruised through my other female ancestors. This made me think about the family tree, a beacon of genetic research today.

The interest in genealogy is a growing field not only among the scientific community but it has become popular with laypeople as well. Different internet sites advertise companies that can trace one's ancestry all the way to the distant past. I sent my saliva to one of these companies and laughed when the result came back connecting me to Marie Antoinette, born in Austria and crowned as the last queen of France before the revolution. My mother's lineage, as far as I know, was of the peasant class and her ancestors lived in an area adjacent to Austria. It is quite possible that one of my great-grandmothers worked as a maid in the Austrian court and caught the eye of a nobleman. Their affair produced a female offspring that carried that first corrupted gene. I find the discovery of my aristocratic ancestry amusing and it has become an entertaining topic during dinners with friends.

On the other hand, some people dig deep into their family's history finding the names and dates of births and deaths of family members of centuries long gone – great-grandparents, married and single aunts, uncles, and countless cousins. Some of them died at birth; the others lived longer, but the most puzzling thing about their passing is the unknown cause of their demise. Even their death certificates don't specify cause of death. Thus, the self-appointed family tree restorer is unable to trace across generations the trajectory of that single eccentric gene that blemished an otherwise perfect family health chart. Military records are also useless in this matter because they only contain names of those relatives killed in different battles and wars but not the information about physical and mental disorders they might have had before their death. It remains unknown if a certain gene perished with them, or they had already passed it on. The ancestral demise due to drunken saloon brawls and gun fights serve only to spice up the narrative of the family lore. Each subsequent generation adds different details to the stories to make them more suitable to the times in which they are told.

The application of 21st century genealogical DNA tests have helped family historians finally to trace the origin of that darn bad boy gene. Mystery solved. Everyone rejoiced knowing that daily breakfast of bacon and eggs didn't elevate their cholesterol; neither did a box of Oreos eaten after dinner cause their diabetes; nor did hours-long playing online games make them nearsighted. Today's family tree templates available online ease the job of the family genealogist because they only include places and years of descendants' births and deaths. The new owners and manipulators of our corrupted gene are medical genealogists. They know us better than we know ourselves because they can follow the gene's long journey as it skips a generation or two, then causes a health crisis in the third one.

Once the template's boxes are neatly completed and the copies of it distributed among family members, the eccentric gene takes center stage.

Its properties are widely discussed and diverse dilemmas surface. For example, what causes Aunt Millie's debilitating migraines, grandma's goiter despite her using iodized salt, and Uncle Jack's protruding belly? Aunt Millie attributes it to his daily six pack of Heineken, but he blames that disgraceful gene for making him lust for beer. Each family tree provides years' worth of questions and answers regarding the genetic profile of a single family member. For some strange reason the impact of a negative gene takes precedence over the positive one. When one is happy, no one praises the joy-gene embedded into his or her DNA. The genetics set aside, I find the family tree to be the most fascinating, entertaining, and endearing of all trees because it safeguards the memory of long-lost relatives and those we personally knew, thus making us cognizant of our past being deep-rooted in our present.

I could easily draw my family tree because it would include only five generations: my maternal and paternal great-grandparents, my grandparents, my parents, my aunts and uncles, and my cousins. Unfortunately, I never gathered the complete information about the places and dates of birth and death of my great-grandparents, neither from my grandparents nor my parents. I am also missing data about my cousins who passed in the last five years. By living abroad, I was unable to attend their funerals. Consequently, my family tree would be incomplete unless I were able to find the missing facts. I am not sure that my children and grandchildren would be interested to learn about their ancestry's life span; thus, I continue postponing my genealogical search. On the other hand, they occasionally ask me from whom they inherited myopia, cholesterol, and freckles.

"Your grandparents' faulty genes reached you!"

Lake Maggiore

The balcony of my third-floor room in the Hotel Des Iles Borromee faced Lake Maggiore, the second largest lake in Italy. The hotel had an elaborate wrought iron vintage railing that could be found in other hotels built in the second half of the eighteenth century. Des Iles Borromee was built in 1863. The hotel located in Stresa, a charming, small town on the lake's shore, offered a breathtaking view of Lake Maggiore encircled by lush green high mountains. The lake didn't emit the salty scent of the Adriatic Sea that I was used to; instead, the fragrance of magnolias spread throughout the area permeated the air with their lemony overtones. I left the balcony door ajar to let the sound of the night waves breaking on the sandy beach enter the room. Their lapping made me long for the impossible, for that man gone from my life a long time ago. I lay in bed under the soft white sheets looking at myself in the mirror fastened to the front of an antique armoire standing on the opposite wall. The reflection of a middle-aged woman didn't face me. Rather, I felt weightless and free, owning my nostalgia without regrets.

The six days that I spent at the lake were short and long at the same time because they were packed with new experiences from day trips discoveries to Milan and the Borromeo 17th century palace, to going on a leisurely boat ride across the lake, to strolling through Stresa's narrow streets lined with souvenir shops. I was able to fend off the departure anxiety until the last day of my stay at the lake. Then it overwhelmed me with the same intensity as if I were already sitting in a taxi driving me from Zagreb airport to my parents' apartment. I felt that my conflicting emotions of eagerness and dread to see them had already burst my bubble of contentment. Somehow, they always succeeded in making me feel guilty for something I had done wrong in the past, according to them but unbeknown to me. I envisioned them opening their front door and greeting me with their usual sour smile that would lead to their reprimands a few minutes later. The memory of my days at Lake Maggiore became therapeutic.

An Afternoon Stroll

The sun was at its zenith as I was crossing the open market. Half of the vendors had already left their wooden stands, leaving behind plums, apples, pears, peaches, and mandarins that spilled over the edges onto the cement floor. Sweepers began to clean up under and around those stands to get them ready for the next day. The other half of the vendors were trying to sell what was left of their produce and fruit by calling on customers to taste slices of large watermelons and halved peaches. The late arriving buyers knew that they could negotiate a lower price because the farmers didn't want to take back their produce because in the summer heat they would rot by the following day. I slowly weaved between banks, inhaling the intoxicating aroma of unspoiled earth bounty. Everyone focused on the purpose of their being at the market, except me, I was a passerby. I tried to spot the exact location of Sveti Josip (*St. Joseph's*) Church, whose belltower rose behind the tall Nama supermarket.

I crossed the street, and the market's buzzing sound was amplified by cars honking, bicycles ringing, and the brakes of tramways screeching. The church's main entrance and side door were wide open. I entered. The pews were empty. The walls were unadorned, painted white, and plain glass covered the windows. I dipped my fingers into the holy water, trying to remember the words that accompany the signing of the cross. It was the second-long lapse of my memory. It must have happened because of some deep-seated emotional attachment to the church that I was entering for the second time in my life. The first time was 75 years ago when my godparents brought me in as a four-month-old infant to be baptized. Nobody ever described that event to me except to point out that my parents were absent because they were government employees at the time. Their attendance would jeopardize their jobs because practicing one's faith, in their case Catholicism, contradicted the Party's antireligious ideology.

I saw a sign above the altar written in large letters: *Dobrodošli u Sveti Josip* (Welcome to St. Joseph's). In a new democratic Croatia, and a member of the EU, everyone is welcome to any place of worship. Catholic churches are brimming with parishioners, catechism is taught in public schools, and politicians cross themselves whenever the TV cameras are on, or photo opportunities present themselves. In thirty years following the Croatian War of Independence, former atheists became fervent devotees of scripture. I took a photo of that slogan because I wanted to show it to my children and grandchildren. I was planning to give them a brief history of the church and explain the symbolic meaning of that welcoming invitation. I am not sure that they would be interested listening to my lecture; I should just give them the link and let them decide what to do with it. Those of you who want to know, the church was built on cornfields called *bugarije* (Bulgarian gardens) in 1934.

I approached the altar, crossed myself again, and prayed for the health and happiness of my children, grandchildren, my husband, my daughter-in-law and her family, my extended family, and my friends. Before exiting I asked the Almighty to grant me good health so that I can take care of those mentioned above, following my instinctual feeling of thinking of myself as being stronger than others, both mentally and physically. I could be wrong, but believing is seeing. I have lived through some tough experiences that would crush most people but left me only bruised, and I quickly bounced back to my usual positive self. I stepped out of the side door and the scorching heat overwhelmed me. The summer of 2023 was one of the hottest ever recorded globally.

I turned right and began to walk on the street whose name was on the plaque I recognized but nothing else. I wasn't surprised; I had seen it the last time some fifty years ago. Older and newer structures lined the street on both sites. Small family size homes with fenced in front and backyards were gone. Each multi-floor house had either a bar, a cafe, a restaurant, a hairdresser's salon, or a different repair shop at the street level. I took a photo of Domino's Pizza with an outdoor seating area under huge white umbrellas. I remembered that at the end of that street, on the left side, there used to be a Winter swimming pool called Mladost

(*Youth*) where our elementary school gym instructor used to take us once a week to teach us how to swim. Most of the kids didn't know how, but I was already a good swimmer because I used to spend one of the summer months on the Adriatic Sea when my parents had a vacation. The only thing I never mastered, either then or when I was older, was diving into the pool. One of my classmates, a tiny blonde girl, a nonswimmer, got it the first day we were there. She had trouble emerging from the water, and our teacher had to rescue her.

In the classroom the two of us sat together on a bench attached to a heavy wooden desk. We were supposed to lean on its back with our hands crossed behind our backs. The teacher told us that this was good for our posture. I have a photo of the two of us taken on the first-grade picture day. In it her broad smile shows her two front teeth missing, her shoulder-length blonde curls held in place with a hairpin on her nape, and her bangs reaching her eyebrows. I found out from another classmate that she didn't continue her education after middle school. Instead, she began to help her mother run a small downtown shop that sold gaudy jewelry and colorful buttons.

The pool built in 1958 did not have a fountain with a sculpture of a swimmer in a diving position in its center that I noticed while recognizing the unchanged entrance to the pool. From the outside the structure kept its original look, which made me happy. It must have been designed to withstand natural disasters and the new democratic government plan to replace landmarks inherited by the past regime. The pool didn't infringe on the sensibility of their new urban aesthetic. I sat for a while on a bench across the entrance browsing through my memory landscape. I remembered the girls' home-made cotton bathing suits and the shabby towels that our mothers sent with us because the better ones would be ruined if by accident they fell in the heavily chlorinated water.

I took several photos of the pool's structure from different angles. A man in his forties sat on a bench nearby following my repositioning while taking them. I am sure that he was wondering why such an interest in an unattractive old building. He wouldn't understand even if I explained it to him because the pool did not belong to his past; it was just an object that he looked at while passing by or resting on the bench, an unanimated entity that left him indifferent. For me it was a part of the topography of my childhood that waited for my return for sixty-eight years. I call that patience.

The pool is situated at the end of Žajeva Street, which got its name from one of the founders of the KPH (Communist Party of Croatia), Andrija Žaje, and replaced the former Daničićeva Street name (Đuro Daničić, 1825 -1888, a Serbian linguist) in 1993. I find the timing of these renamings peculiar because they took place in the middle of the Croatian War of Independence, which ended in 1995 with the declaration of independence from the Socialist Federal Republic of Yugoslavia. One of the reasons that Croats fought that war was the establishment of a democratic statehood no longer governed by an autocratic leadership and its communist ideology. 1993 was also the year when the UN Security Council passed Resolution 827, formally establishing the International Criminal Tribunal for the former Yugoslavia political leaders, mostly Serbs, and prosecuting them for war crimes. In other words, erasing the old and stepping into a new reality in the making was not a painless process for those who had enjoyed the perks offered in the old system. They looked with nostalgia to those times and tried to hang on to mementos of their youth. They changed the names of the streets, squares, and public places in Zagreb (the Croatian capital), some even multiple times, thus confusing not only cabbies but also their clients. It seems that those who implemented the renaming process never understood that the past follows us into the present, thus cannot be obliterated. People tend to undermine both old and new names. Instead, they remember city landmarks, walking in the summer on the hot sidewalks of barren streets, trees in the park changing across seasons, and a first kiss on one of the benches.

I reached the end or the beginning of Žajeva Street and began to stroll on the right side of the street. I remembered that returning from the swimming pool I always walked on that side because my house stood there. I didn't recall any trees on either side of the sidewalks, but there they were, fully grown oaks, probably planted after my parents and I moved to downtown Primorska Street when I was in seventh or eighth grade. I tried to remember the number of my house, and suddenly the number 27 popped up in my head. I first recognized the house next to mine, the identical three-story structure painted bright yellow. My house had a light gray façade with the second-floor balcony railing showing signs of its longevity. The window of our combined bedroom/living room was next to it. Our apartment had a balcony reachable from the kitchen that overlooked the cement courtyard. I stared at that window wondering how many families built their lives in that tiny living space. I am sure that I was the only one born in it, which was a rarity for urban women in 1948. My mother told me that her gynecologist recommended a home birth because of infections that spread throughout the city's maternity wards at that time.

I still remember the interior of our apartment. In order to keep the multifunctional room warm, my mother would hang a colorful Turkish patterned large woolen rug on the wall facing east and exposed to the weather elements. Instead of another house leaning against ours, there was an open space with a small hill where we kids used to go tobogganing. There were also the Turkish-designed, wood-carved small table with two matching chairs, two wider than standard single beds one of which I shared with my father because the room was too small for an additional bed, the coffee table covered with a doily that my mother crocheted, and two oversized upholstered arm chairs on each side of it. The apartment was homey despite its size and uneven heating that depended on the amount of wood logs burning in the kitchen's cast iron stove spreading warmth throughout the rooms. Those were the '50s in the former Yugoslavia when nobody connected the have-nots with poverty because most urban families lived in similar conditions.

I noticed a newly built contemporary house adjacent to mine whose construction was at the same level as the hill. It was one floor taller than the four buildings that one time stood alone facing each other across the street. Its large windows and imposing glass entrance contrasted my house's narrow, graffiti-covered wood panel entrance door with the old-fashioned black knob and the rusty keyhole below it. Clearly neighbors were not scared of being robbed; thus, they didn't care that the keyhole was unusable. There was nothing of great value in their apartments that would attract thieves, as if the '50s never left. I remembered that when we lived there, the entryways used to be locked in the evenings to make sure that the local drunks would not urinate behind them on their way home from the local bar. I took a photo of my house and colorful graffiti on the main door.

I wondered if any of the neighbors who had passed away left their apartments to their children and grandchildren to keep the neighborhood's history alive. Not coming across any of my contemporaries, I guessed that they must have moved elsewhere. I remembered several neighbors my mother's age—a woman from the first floor who had a balcony reachable from the courtyard on which she grew rare cacti. We kids would wait till one of them bloomed and would pull off its single flower with a stick. She was too old to chase us, and we would hide under her balcony where she couldn't see us. The third-floor neighbor, Fanika, was my mother's principal collocutor for the afternoon coffee klatch. Her husband was a sailor and absent for several months on each of his overseas trips, so she raised their son, a ballet dancer, and a daughter, a secretary, alone. One time, I overheard her telling my mother:

"I like it when my husband is away. When he returns, it feels like having a stranger in my house who only needs his laundry to be washed."

She also convinced my mother not to have more children because she knew how hard it would be for her to raise two. I think that she was right, my mother would have been overwhelmed.

Revisiting my past on that hot September day made me happy realizing that Žajeva underwent only minor changes throughout the decades and that the feeling of belonging to it resonated with me. My house is still where I had left it, and the street extends all the way to the train overpass that I used to walk under on my way to elementary school.

"How was your outing?" my husband asked me when I returned to my parents' third apartment in Zagreb's *Stara Knežija* (Old Knežija).

"It was fantastic. I found what I was looking for!"

He looked puzzled expecting to hear more details.

"My street exists, and I saw my house!"

"So?"

He didn't understand that I found what I thought was lost — I found a part of myself.

Downtown

Early afternoon, sunny September in Zagreb. I descended from the tram number 14 at the HNK (Croatian National Theater). I crossed Savska Street with two other people in front of me who impatiently waited for the light to change to green. They were in a rush, while I had all the time in the world to revisit parts of downtown where my parents moved from Daničićeva, today's Žajeva Street.

I first wanted to pass by my elementary school on Kršnjavoga Street that housed students from the first to the eighth grade. The school system in the former Yugoslavia did not have preschool, elementary school, and middle school grade divisions as in the USA. I took a look at the black glass plaque hanging on the right of the massive entrance. I read the school's name written in gilded letters—Izidor Kršnjavi (1845 – 1927), a known Croatian art historian, a university professor, a painter, and a politician. When I attended this school in the '50s it bore the name of Ivo Marinković, who fought in the Yugoslav Front of World War II and was killed in 1943. He was declared a national hero. In the postbellum period, many schools, factories, sport facilities, different institutions, squares, and streets were renamed and given names of those fallen fighters for the liberation from the Nazis. Fifty years forward, the old became new again. Most of the original names were reinstated, and those associated with the communist regime of the former Yugoslavia disappeared. The new democratic Croatian government believed that forsaking the post-war nomenclature of public places would erase the country's past, but by its ignorance or arrogance failed to understand that the past never stops existing; it always remains an essential part of the present.

I took a selfie below the old/new name of my school. This was the only change that I noticed. The exterior walls were still the same dirty gray color, and the tall wood framed windows along with the main entrance had a dark brown stain that I remember. The school built in the neo-Renaissance style of 1895 looked sturdy and authentic. It was the left wing of the three-part monumental building with its central portion facing a square and the right wing extending into the adjunct street called Klaičeva.

I continued my walk on Kršnjavoga Street, no changes there. On my right was the sport field with a running track and two soccer goal nets. I saw several students running and laughing. On my left I passed by a row of old plane trees whose white half-peeled bark I remember well. I turned around the corner to reach Klaičeva Street that led me to Primorska, the street on which I lived for seven years.

Our two-bedroom apartment was number 31, in a three-story structure built in the '30s. I crossed the street to take a photo of it. Each bedroom had one window that seemed to me even closer to the sidewalk than I remembered. Both were about a meter above the pavement enabling passersby to have a clear view into the rooms. The white painted iron bars still covered the windows, and nontransparent curtains protected the privacy of the dwellers. I recalled my mother leaving the bars ajar in one of the bedrooms and putting a metal milk can between them so that the farm woman coming from a nearby village in the predawn hours was able to pour fresh milk into it. Sometimes the noise from the can brushing against the bars would wake me up.

At the end of Primorska Street I recognized a building that provided accommodations for nuns from the nearby church Sveti Blaž (*Saint Blaise*) and retired professionals. In it lived a chubby, gray-haired professor of French and English, Miss B., from whom I took an hour-long lesson once a week. She must have been in her late seventies, possibly younger, but her dentures made her look older. I would stare at them when she would pronounce some English words because they would move making a bit more saliva form in her mouth. For some reason she didn't have any trouble saying French words. I learned very little during those lessons because my teenage brain was planning fun times with my friends instead of focusing on my teacher's grammar explanations. To make my progress even more impossible was the fact that I never did the homework she assigned. Knowing that she would not go over it made it easier to not do it. I was certain that she forgot which exercises I was supposed to complete. I didn't mind those lessons with Miss B. because she was kind and certain that I had a great talent for learning foreign languages. I am sure she told that to my mother to convince her that the money she was paying her was well spent. I also remembered that she seldom smiled, like those people who think being serious enhances their sense of self-importance. Being clownish would make them look less professional. Miss B. did not belong to that category. She just felt that grinning was not necessary for a successful lesson.

I entered Sveti Blaž Church and marveled at how richly decorated it was. The colorful stained-glass windows showing different biblical scenes cast a magical light on the dimly lit nave, pews, and altar. A few times I attended Sunday Mass with my grandmother, Anastazija, when she would visit us from Laduč, a village twenty kilometers west of Zagreb. She would fall to sleep halfway through the sermon. I would rest my head on her shoulder and listen to the priest reading passages from the Bible. They sounded interesting, but I didn't understand their relevance because my parents didn't send me to the catechism that Sveti Blaž organized for the neighborhood kids. They also didn't attend church. Religious beliefs under communism were considered reactionary and incompatible with the system's ideology.

When I exited the empty Sveti Blaž, I faced the southern part of Primorska. Across from it I recognized the one-story old tobacco factory still painted in a dull orange shade. Its structure resisted the tooth of time but seemed vacant, probably looking for a new owner and to be repurposed. Behind it stood a tall, imposing, all-glass office building as a reminder that the new had begun to replace the old. Another sign of the accelerated rhythm of modern living was the rows of cars parked on both sides of Primorska. I remembered my father's blue Fiat 750 as being the only automobile parked in front of our house.

The street is still primarily a residential area with a few local businesses. I felt that I owed it to myself to revisit the place of my youth because I didn't want its images to fade into oblivion. Having found Primorska only slightly altered comforted me, but it also made me realize that I have changed more than I thought. Nowadays, I would feel out of place in a semi-cold, two-bedroom, street-level apartment, not knowing any of the neighbors and listening to car engines being turned on in the morning and the owners slamming their doors after returning from work in the afternoon. My American life changed my perspective on urban living—I prefer a grass-covered lawn, my car parked in the garage, and evenly-heated rooms. However, Primorska Street will always hold a special place in my heart. It was the perfect location to reach on foot the main city square, cinemas, drama theaters, cafes, restaurants, open markets, stores, and, most importantly, meet my friends. Those experiences are unforgettable and irreplaceable.

The adjacent street, Gundulićeva, led me to my high school, still considered one of the best in the country. When I attended it, the school had two diverse curricula—science- and math- based and humanities. I heard that the humanities track was abolished some time ago. I watched students exiting in small groups. They were loud, discussing something of importance to them, but I was too far away to hear it. They made me think about my classmates whose careers I followed, thanks to keeping in touch with several of them who in return would inform me about the lives of those with whom I lost contact. I remember the classroom beauty, a mediocre student, who became an internationally recognized mezzosoprano; the tall, chubby, acne-covered boy who sat at the desk behind mine with his smelly feet stretched under my seat who turned out to be a successful movie and theater director; behind him sat a close friend of mine, a bespeckled red-headed avid reader who pursued his passion to become one of the best translators of Polish literature; the slim, tall, blond girl, a daughter of a known politician, studied to be a high school teacher; another one with a beehive hair style popular in the '60s earned a medical degree; the boy with the light-brown curly hair and the charming smile that always stared at the girls' boobs matured into a well-regarded lawyer; the petite, dark-haired girl who traveled to school by train from her nearby Zagreb village who never graduated because our history teacher, the puffy-faced drunk with rotting teeth, flunked her and she ended up selling produce and fruit on the open market; the girl with whom I shared a desk, got her degree in Italian and worked for a local newspaper, she is my life-long friend and my daily collocutor via email.

We were a unique bunch of young people, baby boomers who liked to exchange ideas, and had heated discussions ranging from politics and culture to sports. We didn't date our classmates because we considered students from other classes more interesting. A group of us founded a small youth theater and there we performed one act plays and skits that two boys from the other class wrote. They both became playwrights after graduating from college. Having been the only girl in the group, I always played the female lead. I mentioned our theater to one of my younger friends twenty years my junior. She was surprised to hear that my generation founded it and said that her generation continued to attend it.

After having taken several photos of my high school's entrance, I headed toward the tram station and waited for the number 14. As I looked through the window passing by known streets, parks, and city landmarks, I wondered why I had such an urge to revisit places of my childhood and adolescence. I couldn't pinpoint just one reason. Sometimes one gets that feeling of doing something at the spur of the moment because of a fear that the same emotion may not be there either tomorrow or ever. Strolling down my memory lane was more than a test of the sharpness of my seventy-five-year-old brain. Having recognized the grounds of my youth gave me a sense of constancy in times when the world is in flux because of clashing ideologies and the relentless pursuit of self-interests. My nostalgia for the past keeps me grounded in the present and helps me navigate through the murky waters of today's global chaos.

Food

Food has a special effect on me. It acts like a self-administrated polygraph test that enables me to be true to myself by legitimizing the existence of diverse sensations that a single meal and a drink can provoke in me. Their color, aroma, and flavor seem to be embedded in both my parietal lobe and my amygdala, areas of the brain which become activated as soon as I have a dish and a glass of mostly red wine in front of me. I soak up their visual, olfactory, tactile, sonic, and even sensual properties. In addition to letting myself dive into the hedonistic pleasure of the moment, they often jolt my core memory of different events, people, travels, and atmospheres that I enjoyed in the past. I have never forgotten freshly baked baguettes in San Martin, a wooden tray with assorted Provencal cheeses in Paris, fried zucchini flowers at Peck in Milan, tequilas in Cancun, oysters in Lim Fjord in Istria, Memorial Day hamburgers, and an Easter brunch at The Ritz Carlton in Dearborn. While sipping my glass of Chianti, I remember friends who also preferred reds, found the Rochefort repulsive, and loved dipping their bread into scampi garlic sauce. The nostalgia for times and many meals we shared is bittersweet because several of my dearest friends have already passed. Everything that connects me to food is permanently stored in my memory bank. On the other hand, trips to the far-away sandy beaches flanked by the turquoise seas, tropical plants and exotic flowers, national parks, and historical landmarks, have become only blurred images stripped of details that once amazed me. They are proof of my selective recall. To feel human, it is important to get to know different people, to have friends, and to share yourself with a heaping plate of spaghetti Bolognese and a glass of Sangiovese.

The Honey

The weather forecast predicted the arrival of a foot or more of snow, fierce winds, and temperatures below zero. Blizzard warnings were issued throughout the morning. Valery looked out of the window in her study and saw blowing snow leaving the trees in the front yard and stripping them of their white coat. A hot cup of green tea warmed her cold hands. She was slowly sipping it and enjoying each gulp because she liked the sweetness of it. Valery always drank any kind of tea by adding a tablespoon of honey. She knew about the medicinal benefits of tea, but that was secondary to the pleasure she derived from the sweet taste it left in her mouth. Furthermore, it would calm her nerves after having to deal with challenges at home and at her job as a real estate agent.

Being a single parent and a professional was a daily juggling act. According not only to her, but also to a myriad of writers, poets, musicians, and known historic and contemporary figures, honey exceeded its therapeutic merits by inspiring the creation of multiple linguistic variations that appeared in different contexts ranging from its daily use to its poetic applications. Honey's easily adoptable properties enabled it to assume diverse metaphoric meanings throughout history because it is a chameleon word that doesn't recognize age, gender, ethnicity, religion, or any other social grouping. The following examples illustrate Valery's point: honeymoon, honeymooners, "Honey, honey," "Honey, I am home," "How was your day, honey?" "Honey, I shrunk the kids," "Honey - bunny, daddy is home," "Honey catches more flies than vinegar," honey trap, honeybunch, honey-do list, honey-mouthed, land of milk and honey, like bees to honey, milk and honey, sweeter than honey, and the list goes on.

Cheesecake's Wanderlust

On a recent visit to Trish, my old friend, agewise and timewise, told me that everyone loved the cheesecake she made for Easter brunch.

"Of course, they did; it's a classic. I can't even count how many times I have used your recipe."

"I don't remember where I got it, do you?"

"I sure do. You had told me that you were invited to dinner at the house of one of Rich's friends in Washington, DC years ago. Your host baked a cheesecake, and you both really liked it. However, he was a total jerk and tried to convince you that you had not seen a white tiger in the local zoo that you visited that same day."

"I forgot about that! God, I am getting senile! How do you remember that?"

"Well, you liked the man's cheesecake, glossed over his insult, and asked for the recipe."

"Good, at least you recall our youth. Are you aware that we have known each other for fifty-two years? They passed in a flick of time, and here we are, two old ladies."

I looked at Trish. She was still trim, laughed loudly and wholeheartedly, and was mentally sharp and politically progressive. Due to spine problems and pain in her right hip, she limps a bit, especially in the evening. She stopped coloring her hair red, too much work, but I continued dying mine dark auburn hoping to shave off a couple of years from my appearance.

"Did you know that since you had given me the cheesecake recipe, I have never again ordered it in a restaurant because it always tasted dry without some kind of sauce poured over it. Ours is perfect, moist, and not too sweet."

Trish's cheesecake recipe has made quite a go around the world. I made it for my Croatian friend when she visited me in the States, and she immediately requested the recipe. The Philadelphia cheese was not available in the groceries in Zagreb at that time; therefore, she replaced it with farmer's cheese and sour cream that she bought on the open market. She later told me that it tasted different but was still wonderful.

The second country in which our cheesecake found a home was Scotland. A daughter of friends of ours ate it when she spent ten days of her spring break in our house. She was an exchange student at the University of Texas in Austin. Years later, married and with two children, she still follows the same recipe. She didn't tell me if she had to alter the ingredients, just that our cheesecake is her family's favorite dessert.

My Brazilian friend Elisa brought the recipe with her when she had visited her family in Sao Paolo. After having a wedge of it, her mother and sisters requested that she write down the ingredients and directions. Our daughter-in-law is equally enamored with the heavenly taste of graham cracker crumbs covered with Philadelphia cheese and full fat sour cream. She prepares it frequently for our son and grandchildren and takes it to their potluck gatherings.

"Trish, can you imagine what an ambassador our cheesecake turned out to be! It also must have a wanderlust built within that makes it happily travel across the globe and carrying a single message—sharing cheesecake is the way to better understanding each other. Who could say no to a pure hedonistic indulgence!"

The original Washington, DC recipe:

CHEESE CAKE

28 squares graham cracker rolling pinned to crumbs
add ¼ lbs. melted butter. Form crust up sides of pan.
16 oz. cream cheese smash in mixer. Add ½ to 3/4 cups
granulated sugar gradually. When fully mixed add 2
fresh eggs one by one and 2 tsp. vanilla. Pour into
crust and bake for 17 minutes at 375 degrees. Cool at
least a ½ hour. Blend by hand 1 pk. sour cream ½ cup
sugar, 1 tsp. vanilla. Pour onto cooled lower portion
Dont break surface. Bake for 5 minutes at 400 degrees